The Worst
Ever?

For my family, with all my love.

This book is dedicated to the next generation, my gorgeous nephews Ethan, Theo, Tulio, Finley and Jake - always follow your dreams and always believe in the Christmas magic!

This is a work of fiction. Names, characters, businesses, places, events and incidents are either the products of the author's imagination or used in a fictitious manner. Any resemblance to actual persons, living or dead, or actual events in purely coincidental.

CHAPTER ONE

It had been a good day. The sun had appeared after a frosty start, and Lee found herself quite enjoying the crisp air and the excuse to wear her new winter coat. She almost felt festive, although she knew her husband Nathan would say she was being ridiculous - there were still six weeks until Christmas, far too early to feel festive.

As she walked to the bus stop, Lee mused that it had been a good day for reasons other than the weather. She had won the case that she had been working so hard on for the past few months, and had enjoyed an after-hours glass of wine with her colleagues at Phillips, Jones and Sharpe to celebrate. At nearly thirty-one, she was the youngest of the three partners in the law firm, but she got on well with the two older women - Gemma Phillips and Tania Sharpe.

Kids had been the topic of discussion in the office that afternoon. Well of course they had - the case had revolved around two children, and both of Lee's colleagues knew she wanted kids sooner rather than later. She had waited for so long - getting through law school, finding a job, working so damn hard to make partner at thirty. She wasn't really sure where she'd found the time to meet a man, to get married - and yet somehow she had. Nathan, luckily, was as married to his job (as a doctor in A & E) as she was - and so despite their conflicting schedules and hectic lives, they muddled along well enough. But kids… they had been on the back burner for a long time, and Lee could feel the clock ticking.

Gemma had regaled them with stories of her new grandson Oliver, and Tania had told stories of the fabulous parties she and her husband had attended. She for one was not interested in having children - she was all about the child-free life.

Despite only being 52, Gemma had grown up children who had begun to have children of their own, and so the three women's lives were vastly different. And even so, they got on like a house on fire.

Finally at the bus stop, Lee sat herself down on the cold, narrow bench and glanced at the digital sign above her head. Three minutes to wait for the bus - and she could be home by half past eight. That was early for her - for the last three months she'd been surprised if she'd been home by half nine. With Nathan on nights every other week, that meant they barely saw each other.

But today was a good day because she'd be home by eight thirty; Nathan was not on nights and she had the takeaway menu hovering in her mind already. A night in front of the telly was definitely what they both needed.

The heavens opened as Lee sat on the bus, but she didn't care - at least she was in the warm and dry and on her way home. She brushed her dark brown hair from her face, and thought that it was getting cold enough to start wearing a hat - although she never liked how her poker-straight hair looked after wearing a hat. Static was not even the word.

She looked out of the rain spattered windows, and yet again felt a tingle of the festive season as the red and white lights from the cars got distorted by the raindrops. She loved this time of year. Whilst not a big fan of Hallowe'en, she was always excited when it arrived for after it she would start to get involved in the festive season. She wasn't sure why she loved it so much; she was the only one in her family who got quite so warm and fuzzy about the holiday time. Her younger sister hated it - complained constantly about the commercialisation, the consumerism, the waste… and Lee knew she had valid points on all those topics. But still, Lee really felt the magic in the winter months. Well, she hated January - when everything was over and yet the dark nights and miserable weather remained. But that build up to Christmas… that was enough to make all of the weather, darkness and money spent worth it.

Lee had loved Christmas for as long as she could remember - even as a child before she had shortened 'Shirley' to Lee and was still being dressed in matching dresses to her sister. And even though her family never found the magic in Christmas that Lee had, it had still been a family event, as she imagined it was in most houses. A massive dinner, beautifully wrapped presents, Christmas films on the television… even her cynical younger sister had not had complaints back then. Well, not until she had found out the truth about Father Christmas, and decided the whole holiday was done for.

While that particular seasonal truth had been disappointing, Lee had never let it dampen her Christmas spirits. In fact, she thought to herself as the bus pulled up outside the house, perhaps she could persuade Nathan to watch a Christmas film that evening. It was, after all, November…

*   *   *

"Nathan!" she called as she let herself in to their two-bedroom Clifton home. She loved it here; from the shiny black door out front to the wooden floors of the hallway; the multi-coloured staircase and the massive king size bed. It was a mixture of modern and old-fashioned: a very modern bathroom with a shower to die for; an aga in the kitchen; a fifty-inch screen in the living room; exposed beams in hallways. It had taken a long time - what with both their work schedules - to get it looking exactly right, but she felt like they'd got there. Inspiration from magazines, the internet, her friends - she'd taken it all on board and created the home of her dreams. Well, their dreams, she supposed. Although thinking about it, she couldn't remember Nathan having much input in the design.

She stood at the bottom of those multi-coloured carpeted stairs and listened for a moment; she could hear the shower running. Heading to the fridge, she pulled out a bottle of white and poured them both a glass, before grabbing the stack of take-away menus they kept on the side. With so many hours put in at work, and decent pay slips to accompany those hours, when the Joneses were home together they often ordered a takeaway. Lee remembered cooking as a kid with her mum, but not much since then… Perhaps at the weekend she would bake something, she thought as she perused the options on the Indian menu.

It was only a few minutes later - when she'd made her choices and was waiting for Nathan to confirm his usual order - that Nathan walked into the kitchen.

"You're home early," he said, reaching over and grabbing the second glass of wine. He was wearing only a towel, wrapped around his waist, and beads of water were still glistening on the dark skin of his chest. His short, dark hair was spiked from being freshly shampooed and the muscles from his thrice weekly gym sessions (which Lee could not understand how he fit in - she was barely awake enough when she got home to talk, let alone work out) were clear in his arms and legs.

"Well hello to you too," Lee said, leaning in for a kiss and tasting the white wine on both of their tongues. It was only brief, but as she pulled away she saw Nathan smile that smile she had fallen for five years ago. Perfect, straight, white teeth and a sparkle in his eye. Unbidden, a thought popped into her head - when did we last have sex? She thought it was concerning that she even had to think about it… things had been hectic lately, but surely it hadn't been that long? She counted back while Nathan told her some tale of his day… three weeks, she thought. Well perhaps that could be remedied tonight.

The takeaway arrived within an hour and - although Nathan pulled a face at the idea of a Christmas movie in November - they spent the evening together on the sofa, catching up on a crime series that they'd started months ago and not got a chance to finish.

"It's nice to be home together," Lee said as she sipped her second glass of wine. She was comfortably full from the curry and naan bread, and was lazily curled up on the grey sofa, leant against Nathan's chest.

"Mmmhmm," Nathan agreed. "It's rare these days."

"I know. I'm sorry."

"I'm not complaining - we're both out a lot."

"And I'm afraid this is a one-off," Lee said. "Next week I start a new case, sounds like it's fairly high-profile - lots of late nights at the office by the sounds of it."

"I'm on nights anyway," Nathan said. "So it doesn't matter."

Lee felt a prick of hurt at the words 'it doesn't matter', but brushed the feeling away; he was right. It was better if he was on nights, because then she wouldn't feel guilty about being out late.

Nathan stretched his long arms and yawned. He'd worked a twelve hour shift from six in the morning, and then put in an hour at the gym on his way home from work. "I think I'm going to head up after this episode."

"I'll come with you," Lee said as the credits ran. She climbed onto Nathan's lap, stretching her skinny work trousers to the limits as she straddled him with a grin. She leant her head until their lips met, and moved her lips with his. She let her fingers run through his now-dry hair and pressed her chest up against him.

Until he pulled away. "I'm exhausted, Lee," he said, looking apologetic.

"Oh. Okay." Lee removed herself from his lap, feeling far less sexy than when she'd climbed on. Indeed, the trousers limited her so much she fell slightly onto the sofa, feeling embarrassed.

It wasn't so much that she was desperate for sex - they weren't newlyweds, she wasn't expecting sex every five minutes. And it wasn't as if she weren't exhausted now - she'd put in her usual thirteen hour day, plus a couple of glasses of wine at work and at home - she was done. But she thought they should at least try…

They followed their usual bedtime routine - one changed while the other used the bathroom, and vice versa. They had never been those people who would use the bathroom together - occasionally they might brush their teeth at the same time, but only when in a real rush.

As they got into their usual sides of the bed and turned the lamps off, Lee shivered a little in the cool air of the bedroom.

"Night," Lee said, snuggling down under the thick winter duvet.

"Good night."

Their backs touching each other, they were asleep in record time, as the hard work of the day took its toll.

CHAPTER TWO

It started off like any other day. Lee got up at the same time as Nathan (the ungodly hour of 5am) and had a lovely, scorching, powerful shower to get herself ready for the day. She dressed while watching the news in the background, leaving her high heels off until the second she walked out the door.

Today she was wearing one of her 'power outfits' - one of three outfits she wore to interviews or particularly important days at work. And today, she thought, justified this power outfit (a skirt suit in navy with a crisp white blouse). After a weekend of relaxing, and a meal out with Nathan to celebrate winning the case, today was the start of a new case. The first high-profile case she had ever led.

The client was a famous soap star, who was in a long, drawn-out and well-publicised custody battle with his equally famous ex-wife. The story had hit all the tabloid papers, as had the astounding news that both parties had left their lawyers and decided to seek new representation. Of course, Phillips, Jones and Sharpe were first on the phone to his 'people', and before she knew it, Lee had ended up as the lawyer in charge of hammering out the details.

Power outfit on, Lee walked carefully down the stairs in just her tights to the kitchen, where as usual she made a large mug of tea and left it to brew while she packed her laptop bag and checked she had everything she needed for the day. Then it was off to the bathroom to put on her make-up, the bedroom to dry and attempt to style her hair (it really did not do anything but poker straight. No matter what she applied to it, what heat she used, it was always poker straight), and back downstairs for a final coat of lip gloss and to slip those high heels on.

Lee got the bus every day, as Nathan took the car and her law firm was in the centre of Bristol, so it made more sense for her to use public transport. The cost of two cars seemed silly, not even considering the environmental impact. Besides, parking in Bristol was never easy - no, the buses were much easier.

Today, however, her bus was late. She could not believe it, as she stood under the thin and dirty plastic shelter, tapping the toe of her beige heels. Not today! The electronic board had told her the bus would be three minutes - eight minutes ago. Now it was stuck on 'due' - and the app on her phone wasn't telling her much different.

This did happen occasionally - 'phantom' buses that never chose to show up, disappearing somewhere into the electronic board's system - but Lee was never usually too stressed by it. She was always in work early - mainly due to the early hours Nathan tended to keep, either getting up or coming home at some horrendous time of the morning - and so a fifteen minute delay was never a huge issue.

But today she knew that her new client would be in at 8:30 and she most definitely could not be late. She looked desperately at the board and considered calling a taxi. But how long would that take?! Never usually one to be indecisive, today she simply could not make the decision. Wait? Call a taxi? Start walking?

Finally, finally, when she had begun to give up hope, the bus appeared around the corner and stopped at her stop. She considered asking the driver where on earth the other bus had vanished to, but took a deep breath and decided against it. It wasn't the bus driver's fault, after all - probably just a technical hitch.

It was as she stepped on to the bus, following her cleansing deep breath, that she heard a crack.

"Surely not…" she muttered to herself, swiping her pass so the disgruntled looking driver could continue on the journey. When she took a step forward, she knew she had been right: the heel of one of her power shoes had broken.

She slid into the nearest seat and pulled off the offending shoe. A clean break, right where the heel met the base of the shoe. How the hell had that happened?

If she were honest, she felt like crying. Rain hit the sides of the bus and no longer did it remind her of the festive period. No, it reminded her that the five minute walk from the bus to her office would be a wet walk.

Thankfully, she kept a pair of thin black pumps in her handbag at all times, and so she switched out the shoes (ignoring how ridiculous it made her outfit look) and thanked her lucky stars that she would at least be able to walk into the office, instead of hobbling in with two different heights of shoes. And tears would not help - she knew that. She pulled out her notes on the high-profile client (Brandon, his name was) and read through them again, wanting to be as prepared as possible when he stepped in to her office.

It was eight o'clock before she stepped in to her office, wet from the persistent drizzle and wearing emergency shoes. She was, of course, well behind Tania and Gemma who got in by half past seven at the latest - as Lee normally did.

They both happened to be stood in the lobby, wondering where she'd got to, when she walked in. They both looked at her, puzzled looks on their faces.

"Please don't," Lee begged. "It's been a nightmare of a morning. Let me go and get myself sorted before Brandon comes."

She knew it was a bit of a coup to get this client herself - to be honest, she had expected one of the others to fight harder for it (despite being good friends, they also all had ruthless streaks when it came to their careers; without them, they would not have made it so far nor so fast in such a male dominated world), and had been over the moon to get this client for herself. It would be one to make the newspapers - one that she hoped to win, for the coverage of 'Shirley Jones, successful lawyer to the stars' would be thrilling to see in print. She imagined how proud her mum would be. She was proud, of course, that her daughter was a lawyer - but being in a newspaper, linked with a soap star that mum was bound to have heard of, now that would really make mum glow. Since dad had walked out on her ten years previously, Lee always aimed to do things that would make her mum happy.

"I think it's a bit late for that," Gemma said. "I'm fairly sure that's him coming up the road!"

"Stall!" Lee shouted, dashing into her office and closing the door. She opened her emergency bottom filing cabinet drawer and took out a hair brush to make her hair look slightly less bedraggled, and some super glue. She fixed the heel as best as she could, hearing her colleagues talking slightly too loudly on the other side of the door as they tried to detain the newest of their clients. She squeezed them together with all her strength, hoping that the few precious seconds would be enough for them to hold her weight. Perhaps she could pretend her office had a standard no-shoe policy… but no, it sounded ridiculous even as she thought it.

Hearing footsteps approaching her door, she threw the spare shoes, super glue and hairbrush back into the cabinet drawer, slammed it shut and slipped the hopefully now fixed heels back on. She held her breath as she slowly walked towards the door, teetering slightly - but magically, they held. Now, she thought, all she needed to do was stand on them long enough until it was acceptable to invite him to sit. Then that would surely give the glue time to dry.

She opened the door to find her colleagues and Brandon stood on the other side, ready to knock.

“Ah, Lee,” Gemma said, clearly pleased that Lee was looking a little more put together than when she’d run in five minutes previously. “This is Brandon Moore. Brandon, meet Lee Jones, your new lawyer!”

Lee put out her hand to shake his; he was wearing a deep blue suit with a matching tie, and had slightly wavy, dark brown hair that fell into his eyes. She remembered from the notes that he was 41, and of course he was divorced. They’d been co-parenting fairly successfully until his ex had decided to marry - and now they were embroiled in a bitter custody battle.

She realised a few moments into her thoughts that she still hadn’t shaken his hand - and he still hadn’t extended it. She lowered her hand and looked at him, slightly confused.

“You’re Lee Jones?”

“At your service,” Lee said, with a slightly awkward smile. She could feel the broken heel wobbling beneath her foot. She hadn’t planned to stand for this long on it.

“Lee Jones, partner of this firm?”

This was just strange now. “Yes…”

And still Brandon did not offer to shake her hand. Instead, he took his phone from his back pocket and walked away.

Lee looked at Gemma, then Tania - and they all looked as nonplussed as she did. Tania shrugged, and the three followed him out to the lobby.

“Lee Jones is a *woman*,” Brandon said into the handset. “I told you, I wanted a *male* lawyer. I’ve had enough of women.”

Lee's eyes widened in shock as she heard these words. He wouldn't work with her because she was *female*?!

Gemma and Tania's faces told the same story - shock, irritation and anger.

"Get me another lawyer. Now." He hit the hang up button harder than necessary and whirled round to face the three women. He had the presence of mind to at least look apologetic.

"Sorry, ladies. But the name - it threw me. I need a male lawyer - so this is not going to work out."

And with that, he walked out of the door - and he'd never even shaken Lee's hand.

"Is he fricking kidding me?" Gemma was the first to speak. "What century are we in?"

Lee stood, dumbfounded, seeing this opportunity pouring down the drain. Perhaps, she pondered, that was why there had been no arguments about who would get the case - he'd asked for Lee.

Because he'd thought she was a man.

What a crappy day - and it was only nine in the morning.

* * *

They discussed this development over coffees in Lee's office for nearly an hour, agreeing that the man was clearly a misogynist, and reassuring Lee that it had nothing to do with her professional capabilities. And she knew that, she really did - but it didn't mean that she didn't feel a crushing disappointment. In this day and age, none of them could believe that a man could walk away from a good lawyer simply because she was a woman - but that was clearly what had happened, and it hurt. Besides, this had been their big opportunity, a way to build up their modestly sized law firm into something bigger. They were doing well - it wasn't like this would be the end of them - but it had been a chance for something more. And now it was dashed in mere moments.

"Right," Tania said, downing the end of her coffee. "We'd best get back to work. Plenty of non-celebrity, non-sexist clients to do work for."

"At least we won't have to work late every night this week, I guess," Gemma said. "My husband will be pleased, at least."

"Mmm," Lee agreed, still feeling annoyance at Brandon's treatment of her in the back of her mind. As her colleagues left the office she began to file some paperwork, and started to prepare for a small case that she was taking to court the following week. She was fairly confident she would win it - and once she'd finished that paperwork she found she had little left to do. She had cleared most of her paperwork in preparation for this new case; again she felt annoyance burn through her at the wasted hours she'd put in prepping. If the man had just bothered to search for her online, he would have known that she was a woman. Not that that should have stopped him from hiring her.

After putting in a couple of calls to potential clients, and checking in with her colleagues, it was almost four o'clock, and she decided for once to leave early. It had been a crappy enough day as it was, she thought - might as well turn it into some sort of positive and get a full evening at home. Besides, Nathan was on nights, which meant that if she were quick she would get an hour or so with him before he headed out to work. Perhaps reconnect a little - something he had been too tired for the night before.

She'd given up with the heels by lunchtime; unfortunately, she thought they were probably a lost cause, and so she was back in the flats that did not match her outfit in the slightest. And actually, she didn't care - she couldn't wait to get home, get out of her stupid power outfit and snuggle up in her pyjamas. In fact, one of the Christmas films that Nathan would roll his eyes at was definitely on the cards.

"See you tomorrow," she shouted down the hallway, and Gemma and Tania replied with their goodbyes - as it hadn't been their case, their workloads hadn't massively altered. Lee glanced back as she opened the front door, feeling a little guilty - but then she pushed that feeling to one side. She never left early and - aside from this morning - was never late. She could take this one early finish for herself. It would wash away her anger at the events of the day and allow her to start again fresh tomorrow, ready to start chasing another big client for the firm.

Running a little because of the never-ending rain, she stepped into the taxi that was waiting outside. This was a luxury she didn't often allow herself - despite decent salaries, Lee was at heart a saver, not a spender - but today she had totally had enough of public transport. Besides, she convinced herself, it was worth the cost to get home in time to see her husband before he left for work. She couldn't remember the last time she had seen him before he went out on a night shift.

The taxi driver was chatty, and so they spent the short journey discussing the weather, the Banksy they passed and the food festival starting the following weekend. She was pleased, when they pulled up, that there were lights on in the house. Good, she thought, he's not left early. Lee paid for the taxi and, wishing she had thought to bring an umbrella that morning, headed up the slippery path to their front door.

Lee slipped her key into the lock and as she did, felt the usual sense of calm that their house brought over her - despite the bad day. She slid off her shoes by the door; normally this was to stop her heels scratching the exposed wooden floors, but she didn't really need to worry about that with her current footwear. Still, she took them off, and glanced into the living room and then the kitchen to see if Nathan was around. She called his name but there was no answer; presuming he was in the shower, she padded around downstairs for a few moments, checking the mail, listening to the answer machine and flicking the kettle on, ready for a nice cup of tea.

When Nathan didn't appear after she'd completed these tasks, she started up the stairs to find him. Perhaps, she thought, she could join him in the shower... That would surely bring some intimacy back. She wasn't sure why, but his rebuffing of her the previous week was bothering her more that she let on. She knew she shouldn't let it; it wasn't like there had never been nights where he had wanted to and it had been Lee who was too tired, or stressed, or had a headache. But still, it bothered her.

The bedroom door was closed, which was in itself unusual, and jarred her slightly. Nathan was generally quite claustrophobic, and it meant he rarely shut doors if he were in a room by himself - and even when they slept, he liked to have the door slightly ajar.

It was as Lee's hand touched the handle that she heard it: a voice. A woman's voice.

Heart racing, brain whirring trying to come up with twenty-five different, innocent explanations for the sound of a woman's voice in her bedroom, Lee dipped the handle down and slowly pushed open the door.

"Oh Nate..." That was the first thing she heard when she walked in, but she almost didn't hear it; what she was seeing was enough to block her senses and make her head scream for her to retreat.

Masses of blonde, curly hair. Smooth, white skin against dark skin. A red and black lacy bra.

The sight of a woman riding her husband.

For a second she was silent, trying to think of something to say, something to do - because this surely was not happening. Surely, surely she wasn't seeing her husband with another woman. They had not seemed to notice her entrance, and so she decided to make them aware of it, by slamming the bedroom door behind her.

She stood there, in front of that pure white door, as the pictures on the wall shook slightly and all activity on the bed ceased.

"Shit. Lee, I-" But Nathan Jones didn't really have any words. What could he say? That it wasn't what it looked like? Of course it was. That was plain to see.

The blonde didn't turn round and face Lee; instead she extricated herself from compromising position, taking the duvet with her, so it was Nathan who lay there fully exposed. Without a word, she wrapped the duvet around her young, pert, naked body and slid into the en-suite, locking the door behind her.

Lee wanted to scream. She wanted to cry. She wanted to throw things. But she just stood there, looking at the naked man who had torn her heart to shreds.

Nathan scrambled for his boxers and a t-shirt, pulling them on without speaking. Perhaps he thought it was better if he were dressed before he defended himself; Lee didn't think there could possibly be any way to make this better. A small part in the back of her brain was proud of her, for not bursting into tears; she felt a cold, icy wave run through her brain as she stood, calm, poised, ready to hear his excuses.

She wanted to throw up.

Unable to bear the thought of that woman in the en-suite, Lee left the room, leaving the door open for Nathan to follow her downstairs. She desperately wanted to pour herself a glass of wine, but thought that she needed a clear head; thought that she may well need to drive later that night. Instead she settled for that cup of tea she'd been looking forward to all the way home.

"Lee..." Nathan's voice entered the room before she saw him. She couldn't look him in the eye; instead she focussed on the other details. Tousled hair, freshly shaved face, crumpled clothing. No, that wasn't any better than that look in his eye.

"How long have you been cheating on me?" Lee asked, concentrating on keeping her voice steady. After all, she was a barrister; she'd had practice at interrogating, as well as defending.

But there was no defence here.

"Lee, it's not like that, it's not some big thing, I promise..."

"Not a big thing? You're shagging some blonde in our bed, Nathan. And we're *married*. You have cheated on me. How long has it gone on for?"

She met his eye now, and watched him squirm and look away. She felt like her whole life was laid out in front of her, nothing quite what it seemed. For no matter how disconnected they sometimes felt, or how many hours they both worked, Lee had always felt their marriage was strong. Stable. Able to withstand their careers and their busy lives.

Obviously she had been mistaken.

"A few months," Nathan eventually admitted.

Shock hit Lee like a train.

"Months?" she eventually whispered. "In... in our home? In our bed?" She could feel her calm crumbling, and all of a sudden the sense of peace she found in their home was dissolving around her. It had been poisoned by what he'd done.

"I'm sorry, Lee," he said, putting his head in his hands and taking a deep breath. "I'm not in love with her, I promise. It's just..."

"Sex?" Lee finished, and he nodded.

"Why?" She couldn't ask a more detailed question - didn't trust herself to get the words out without faltering, without tears.

"I was stressed... we weren't having sex..."

Of course. This was bound to be put back on to her, she thought. Bound to be her fault.

"It just happened one evening. At work. And then..." She looked at him, this man she had loved for so many years, and for the first time ever thought he looked weak.

Lee took a seat on one of the bar stools that surrounded their marble kitchen island - something she remembered being delighted with when it was fitted - and cradled the mug of hot tea in her hands.

"I'm sorry, Lee. It won't happen again..." Nathan said.

"It won't happen again? Nathan, you have ripped apart the trust of our relationship, you have destroyed a five year relationship. And you think you can say sorry and 'it won't happen again' and everything's suddenly fine? Have you lost your mind?" She was shouting now, and she knew it - but she didn't care. His blasé attitude towards the magnitude of his crime was making her furious.

Down the hall, the front door clicked closed, more loudly perhaps than had been intended. Clearly the blonde had left the building.

"Who is she?" Lee asked.

"Just another doctor from work," Nathan said standing awkwardly opposite Lee. At least he was being honest, she thought.

"And is she the only one?"

There was a pause. A pause that was pregnant with so many assumptions.

"Is she the only one?" Lee asked again through gritted teeth - but his pause had been enough to answer her question.

"There was one night… with a nurse. A year ago." Lee wondered if telling her was making him feel better, assuaging his guilt in some way. He didn't deserve to feel better. She wondered if he knew the agony she was feeling in this moment.

And still she stopped herself from crying.

"A year ago…" It wasn't a question; no, it was simply an acknowledgement that their relationship had obviously been broken for a lot longer than she had realised. Irreparably so, perhaps.

"Lee, there's been so many nights where I haven't seen you, where I've left for work long before you come home… and I was weak, and I gave in to that, and I know that was wrong."

"So how can you say it won't happen again?" Lee asked.

"Because I love you." He grabbed hold of her hand and she didn't instantly pull away. There was that familiar warmth; that feeling of being close to someone who you knew inside and out.

Except she didn't. She would never have imagined he would cheat on her - with two different people, on multiple occasions. That would not have even crossed her mind.

"I don't want to lose you Lee - I know I've done something stupid, but if you can forgive me I will do anything I can to make it up to you."

Lee took a deep breath and didn't speak for a few moments, letting her brain whir and process all these things he was saying.

Then she pulled her hand from his.

"It won't work."

"It will! Lee it will, I promise, I'll try harder."

"No, it won't. Because you say you love me now, but I presume you would have said that for the whole last year - and I would have believed you. And yet you have cheated on me for a year." She stood, putting her empty cup in the sink and picking up the car keys from the counter. "I can't trust you."

He didn't say anything to that - but then what could he say? She knew in her heart that everything she said was true. This was poisoned now - as much as she didn't want to believe it, it was ruined. She walked towards the doors, with the car keys in her hand - not asking, just taking. By rights, she should have told him to get out of the house, but it felt as though the house was toxic too, and she needed to be in a fresh space. She didn't grab anything on the way out, other than her coat and her phone; she just wanted to make it out of the house without crying.

"Lee…" His voice called from the kitchen, but she did not wait to hear what he had to say. She made it out the front door, down that slippery path, and into the little silver Citroen that she so rarely drove.

And then it hit her. She'd kept it together until that point, but it was then that the tears fell - hot, fast and angry, beating a path down her face in their race to get out. It was loud and it was ugly - and it helped release a fraction of the hurt she was feeling. She hit the steering wheel in frustration, and shouted a few swear words into the silence of the dark, cold car.

It was five minutes before she regained some sort of control. Pleased she was wearing the flat shoes - even if they had got soaked from the walk between the house and the car - she turned the key in the engine and began to drive. It was half past five and pitch black outside - well, it was November. Unsure of the destination, she revelled in the freedom she felt at driving alone, at night, with no plan. She drove around housing estates, she drove around shopping centres, she drove until the petrol light lit up on the dashboard and she was forced to pull in to a petrol station.

She needed a plan, she thought, as she paid for the petrol, a very large bar of chocolate and a bottle of cheap white wine. The where was the next part of the plan that was needed: a hotel? A friend's house? Most of their friends were mutual, and she couldn't face the humiliation of telling them that her husband had been shagging a blonde doctor, and a nurse of undefined hair colour, for the past year. Her colleagues, she considered briefly, for they were hers and hers alone - Nathan barely knew them, despite all the hours she spent with them weekly.

But the same thought hit her - she'd have to tell them. She'd have to see the shock and pity in her eyes. Her mum? But she was an hour away, and she *loved* Nathan. It would devastate her. She wouldn't want to think of her little Shirley (the name she insisted on calling Lee, despite her protestations) being left alone, just like she had been by Lee's dad. Then there was her sister… that was the most likely option, she thought. Her sister wasn't married, thought Nathan was a bit pretentious (something she'd admitted after one too many glasses of Chardonnay) and would be willing to get drunk and hurl abuse at the idea of Nathan cheating on her sister.

CHAPTER THREE

Forty-five minutes of driving South and she reached her sister's flat in Exeter. She hadn't called first, but hoped that the fact that it was a weeknight would mean that her sister - who was the opposite of Lee in almost every way possible - would be home, and home alone. As far as Lee knew, her younger sister (by two years - she hadn't yet hit the big 3-0 whereas Lee had passed that milestone) wasn't dating anyone - but as she walked up the pathway she questioned her decision to turn up unannounced. To be fair, she hadn't really been in the right frame of mind to think about anything - she just had to do *something*. And so turning up here was what she'd done. She hadn't even brought any clothes, or a toothbrush - although she was hopeful that her sister would offer for her to stay the night.

Taking a deep breath, and trying to push yet again the image of Nathan with *her*, Lee knocked on the door and was quickly face to face with her sister. Both had blonde hair, but that was where the similarities really ended; Elizabeth's was curly where Lee's was always straight; Elizabeth had freckles where Lee did not; Elizabeth was slightly below average height with curves, where Lee was above average height and willowy.

"Lee!" Elizabeth exclaimed, pulling her sister down for a hug before even asking what she was doing there on a random Monday evening.

"Hey, Beth," Lee said with a watery smile. Elizabeth and Shirley; both had chosen to shorten their long and fairly old-fashioned names. Only their mother really called them by the full versions - and the occasional official.

"Come in - is everything okay?"

Lee shook her head, and didn't trust herself to speak. They walked through the hallway, past the clothes horse full of clothing drying by the radiator, and into the living room that was lit with many candles. Without speaking, Lee took off her coat and draped it over the sofa, then handed the cheap bottle of wine to Beth.

And then she burst into tears.

"Lee! Lee, what's the matter?"

Through sobs and struggling to calm her breathing, Lee managed to convey the key points to Beth; Nathan had been cheating on her and she had walked out.

"What a shit," Beth said, and although it didn't change anything, it made Lee feel a fraction better. She knew coming to her sister's had been the right decision; she needed someone to say all the bad things she was thinking.

"What an absolute wanker. Lee, you have always been too good for him, and this has just proved that. How could he do that to you? Here, let me get glasses. You need wine. You're staying, I presume?"

Lee smiled slightly through her tears at her sister's stream of questions and abuse. "Please, if that's okay. I need to think what I'm going to do."

"Of course, stay as long as you need. Right, wine…"

With full glasses of cheap and not particularly cold wine, Lee and Beth began to dissect Nathan's behaviour, and could only come to one conclusion, no matter how late the hour got; his behaviour was despicable.

"If he wasn't happy," Lee said, after they'd finished the wine and started on the vodka Beth kept in, mixed with flat coke, "Then he should have said something. Talked to me. If he thought we weren't having enough sex, he should have used his bloody words and told me! We could have fixed it! Instead he decides to take some floozy to our bed. Our bed, I mean, is he kidding me! We have money, he could have at least had the decency to take her to a hotel."

"And the nurse! And the way he tried to justify it…" This was the third hour of discussing the night's events, and Beth felt she could picture the scene as clearly as if she'd been there.

"I wanted a baby with him," Lee said, suddenly breaking into sad, drunken sobs. "We'd said we'd talk about it soon, and all along he was sleeping with other people…"

"Oh Lee…" Beth put her arms around her older sister and tried to think of the words that would make things better. "Things will get better. It's better you know now, than for it to just keep going on behind your back. You'll get through this - I promise."

Lee nodded, wiping away the tears that kept flowing from her eyes.

"I'm sorry to dump all this on you. And I know you've got work tomorrow…"

"Don't be ridiculous," Beth said, running a hand through her curly hair as she glanced at the clock; nearly two in the morning. "What are you doing about work tomorrow?" she asked gingerly. She knew how important Lee's job was to her - but she also knew there was no way she could go and face clients in this state.

"Call in sick," Lee said, and Beth was a little shocked. She thought it was the first time she had ever heard her sister even mention skipping work - let alone actually doing it!

“Good plan. I’ll do the same - I think the hangovers we will have tomorrow will make it true anyway,” she said with a chuckle. “And the office will survive without me, I’m sure.”

“No-one wants me…” Lee slurred. “A big client walked out yesterday because I was a woman. He thought I was a man because of the name…” She hiccoughed at the end of her sentence, and Beth - who it seemed could handle her alcohol better than her big sister - decided it was time for bed.

“It’s simple, Lee - all men are pricks. Come on, let’s get you to bed.”

Lee nodded, agreeing with both of her sister’s statements. Beth led her into the spare bedroom which was made up with blue floral bedding, and put a large glass of water on the bedside table. She felt her sister would need it at some point during the night. Although she had planned to dig out some spare pyjamas for her, she thought it was unnecessary - Lee pulled back the covers and climbed in fully clothed, still wearing her make-up, her eyes drifting closed as soon as her head hit the pillow.

Beth pulled the covers up over her sister’s shoulders and stroked her straight, dark blonde hair from her eyes. She kissed her on the forehead and whispered: “Sleep well, sis. It’ll look better in the morning.”

*   *   *

Although Lee fell asleep almost instantly she unfortunately did not stay that way. By three in the morning she was wide awake with a dry mouth, a headache and a sick feeling that did not wholly come from over-indulging on alcohol. She downed the glass of water that Beth had kindly left for her and lay for a long time, staring at the ceiling, wondering what had become of her life. The perfect job, the perfect house, the perfect marriage… it was all falling down around her, and she felt like her mind couldn’t deal with all the changes she knew were coming. After a long time staring at a hairline crack in the white ceiling above her, she rolled over and rifled around in the handbag next to the bed to find her phone. It only had 6% battery, but she didn't think she'd brought a charger with her. She'd deal with that in the morning.

2 missed calls. 1 message.

All three were from Nathan. Lee didn't even bother to read the message; there was nothing that could be said that would make this situation any better. Besides, in her foggy, slightly drunk, slightly hungover brain, Lee had a fuzzy thought that three attempts to get hold her was a bit pathetic. He'd cheated, and she'd left - surely he could have tried harder? She hoped to god he hadn't rung her mum, or her colleagues - but then if he did, he would have to admit what he'd done, and none of the three women would respond well to that bombshell. No, Lee thought Nathan would be too cowardly to admit that particular nugget of information to anyone.

So that she didn't have to think about it in the morning (well, later in the morning than it already was), Lee opened up her emails and drafted something simple to Tania and Gemma to explain her absence.

Hiya - had an awful stomach bug all night and can't stop being sick, so I won't be in tomorrow. Sorry - Lee x

It wasn't long before she had a reply - it said a lot about their jobs that 3am replies to emails weren't that shocking. They weren't the norm, but they certainly weren't unusual.

Don't want to sound heartless, but this isn't anything to do with how Brandon treated you, is it? Please don't let his misogyny affect you - you're a brilliant lawyer. Tania x

Lee closed her eyes for a moment, but opened them again when she found the room beginning to spin. No, this wasn't because of

Brandon; she would have gone into work the next day ready to find another big client - if, that was, her husband hadn't turned everything she knew upside down.

No, she reassured Tania. *Just a stomach bug - honest. Hopefully only twenty-four hours. Will let you know.*

She rolled over, keeping her eyes open to avoid the spinning, and knew that the sickness she felt in the pit of her stomach was going to last a lot longer that twenty-four hours.

It was six in the morning when Lee decided to get up. It was no use lying there, thinking about all the ways her life was ruined. How her favourite time of year was coming up and yet she did not have a husband she could trust, a beautiful home or even a job she was feeling happy in at this moment.

No, Lee decided there was no use lying there, mulling over what could have been. It was time for action; never mind that she didn't know what that action was.

She didn't need to dress - after all, she had never undressed, and she had nothing to change into. Borrowing Beth's toothbrush, she tried to make herself a little more presentable for whatever today would bring. Then she scribbled a note to her sister, grabbed her handbag and her now dead phone, and headed out to the car.

* * *

By the time Beth woke up, with a slightly sore head if truth be told, and read her sister's note, Lee was long gone.

Thanks for the wine and words of advice. I needed to do something - I don't know what - but I'll let you know once I've made any decisions. Love you always. Lee x

* * *

The open road lay ahead of her as she exited the little village outside of Exeter. She liked the quiet of the roads at this time in the morning; she felt a sense of freedom at knowing her phone was off and no-one could contact her. She knew at some point, people would start to worry - she'd have to make contact before then. She found she didn't really care if Nathan worried - but her colleagues would need some sort of excuse if she wasn't going to be in tomorrow.

Pushing the accelerator to the floor, she sped down the motorway, heading further South, trying to leave her broken heart behind. While the distance did nothing to lessen the pain she felt, she did feel a little thrill at doing something spontaneous.

She drove for nearly an hour, stopping at a small services in the hope of picking up a phone charger. She was in luck; they had them on special offer if you bought £30 of petrol. Despite enjoying the freedom of no contact, she knew she would need it before the day was out - wherever she ended up.

As she purchased her petrol, phone charger, a toothbrush and some more chocolate, she wondered if she'd gone mad. Left home, left her sister's, drive to the middle of nowhere with no plan, no phone charger - not even a clean pair of knickers. It certainly sounded like she had gone mad. If anyone else had told her this story she would have definitely thought they had lost the plot, had a breakdown - probably some sort of euphemism.

But the truth was, in spite of not knowing where the journey would take her, her mind felt clearer that it had in at least twenty four hours - possibly more. The more she thought as she drove, the more she felt as though she had sleep walked through the last few months - or maybe longer - of her life.

The M5 became the A38 and whilst there were still two lanes and a seventy mile an hour speed limit, there were suddenly hills and sharp bends that she wasn't used to navigating. She slowed a little, trying to remember when the last time she had travelled this far South had been. Five years ago, she thought - she, Beth and her mum had taken a trip together to a little town called Dartmouth, with brightly coloured houses and breath-taking views. Perhaps she could head there again… or perhaps somewhere completely new.

Would she go to work tomorrow? She thought it was unlikely - she was surely two hours from home and had no desire to turn back. Besides, she didn't really have a home. Not anymore…

No. That was a dangerous path. To take her thoughts from their present direction, Lee took the next exit from the dual carriageway and slowed considerably as the lane became a single one and the thick trees blocked out much of the dim November morning light.

It felt like she'd driven for a long time on windy roads, over narrow bridges and past small, brick houses, when in truth the clock told her she had only been driving for twenty minutes - the unusual driving conditions just made it seem longer, she supposed.

It was then that she saw the sign: "*Welcome to Totnes.*" And beneath it, in black graffiti read: "*Twinned with Narnia.*"

Twinned with Narnia? She mulled that over in her mind. It certainly sounded like an adventure…

CHAPTER FOUR

Compared with where she lived, it was a tiny town; she was surprised to see it had a train station. It didn't take her long to follow signs to a car park, and as she rooted around in her handbag she was relieved to find she had enough change to pay for the machine. It was less than she was expecting, anyway.

Totnes. She didn't think she'd ever heard of it before, but she thought it was worth a look around. Besides, last night's dinner had consisted of a chocolate bar, wine and vodka, and she was starting to feel very hungry. Some lunch (or late breakfast, she supposed), and then she'd decide what to do. Maybe she'd stay the night - that would shock Nathan, wouldn't it, if he couldn't get hold of her and no-one knew where she was.

Or maybe he'd just spend the night with the blonde. Maybe he wouldn't care at all…

A weak winter sunshine was beginning to break through the clouds, and Lee couldn't help but notice how different the weather was here to the lashing rain she had been so late in yesterday morning in Bristol. Was that really only a day ago? It felt like a lifetime.

Lee took her time, wandering slowly past pretty window displays and a group of people protesting the opening of a large chain coffee shop. A little bemused, she took a leaflet, thinking it was something she could read with her lunch - after all, she had no phone to read, and no company.

It was the bright green shutters that caught her eye; an emerald green really with rose covered curtains behind them. Outside were wooden tables and chairs in various shades of green and blue; inside she could see a stand of mouth-watering looking cakes and another five or six tables. Suddenly her stomach growled, and that peckish feeling turned in to full on hangover hunger. Just like the rest of her actions that day, she didn't think - she just walked in.

"Take a seat dear, I'll be right over," the small, grey haired lady behind the counter said. Lee rustled up a smile and chose a table in the window, next to those flowered curtains, where she could look out and see the world passing her by.

"Here's a menu, breakfast is served for another half an hour," the lady announced. "Can I get you a drink?"

"Tea, please," Lee said, perusing the menu and trying to decide what she fancied.

As she did so, she let her mind wander a little, hearing all the sounds of the café around her. The steam from the coffee machine; the buzz from the fridge; the chatter between the waitress and her next customer.

"I'll miss you, Val, you know that," the customer was saying.

"Oh give over. You'll forget all about me as soon as someone else takes over."

"But what if they don't! You're the best in town, and you know that. Besides, if it closes down permanently I'll never make it to one of those places at the top of the hill, not with my knee."

"Totnes is as busy as ever, Ethel. I'm absolutely positive someone will come and take over the lease. It was only advertised a couple of weeks ago, you've got to give it time!"

Lee let their voices swim in an out of their mind, finding that their accents were quite strong and different to what she was used to hearing. She decided to have the pancakes for her breakfast, and they arrived quickly, along with her tea. There seemed to be no rush to leave; no-one was waiting for her table, and she found herself feeling a little sleepy after her lack of sleep and now with a full stomach.

She pulled out the leaflet and began to scan it as the waitress cleared up around her. “Keep Totnes independent,” it read. “No to tax dodgers.” “Keep shopping local!” One thing was for certain, Lee thought - this town certainly had personality.

* * *

It was half an hour later before Lee stood at the bottom of the high street and looked up the steep hill of shops. Christmas lights had been hung, although she presumed they hadn’t been lit yet, but were just waiting for the festive season to truly begin. Clothes, she thought - no matter what happened, she needed some clean underwear and a fresh top before she headed back to Bristol. She also thought she should plug her phone in and tell work she was still ill - there would be no law work for her tomorrow.

“Excuse me,” a sudden voice came from behind her. “Excuse me. Blind workshop coming through.” Blind workshop? Lee jumped out the way, sure she’d heard wrong. Four people followed a guide, and each of them wore a black blindfold and held their hands in front of them. Lee shook her head slightly, wondering if she were imagining things - but no, this was really happening. For a fraction of a second she turned to her right, about to look at Nathan in disbelief, before she remembered she was here alone.

Rooms available tonight! A sign said in the window of the opposite pub. And, just like the rest of her decisions today, her mind was made for her - she would spend the night in this quirky little town, buy some clothes, have some dinner, and head back home tomorrow. It was just what she needed to get her mind in order before she went home to sort her affairs - or, should she say, her husband’s affairs.

The small pub had two single rooms and two doubles available immediately, and Lee decided to splash out on the double, despite being alone - might as well enjoy her night of freedom. She was pleased to find it was clean, equipped with a small en-suite and tea and coffee making facilities. She glanced at the sixties style analogue clock above the door - 11am. She had the whole day ahead of her. The crisp, white sheets caught her eye, and she decided to do something she'd not done since she was a student in her second year of university; she decided to have a nap. Closing the thick curtains to block out the light, and plugging in her phone (although not bothering to switch it on), Lee slipped between the sheets fully clothed for the second time that day and let her eyes flutter closed. It was gone three in the afternoon before she began to stir.

*   *   *

For a second when her eyes opened, Lee didn't remember where she was. Momentarily she thought she was in her Clifton house, asleep under her thick duvet beneath the exposed beams. Then she realised that, while there were exposed beams above her, they were much darker - and this definitely wasn't her home. It hit her then, like a truck - the betrayal, her life in ruins around her, her mad actions leading her to sleeping in the daytime in a B&B above a pub. She groaned into the pillow and asked herself - not for the first time that day - what she was doing.

As she crawled out of bed feeling a little better for the long nap, Lee caught sight of herself in the mirror. She was pleased the shops would still be open - she *had* to get some clean clothes, and a hairbrush. Oh, and some food, she thought, as her stomach grumbled noisily.

As a concession to all the things she didn't have, Lee brushed her teeth with the toothbrush she had picked up in the petrol station and waited for her phone to load now that it was fully charged. As soon as it had turned on, it began to buzz like an angry wasp as missed calls and messages flooded in. Taking a deep breath, Lee threw it into her bag, determined to get to the shops before they closed, and vowed to face the messages over dinner.

It was amazing, she thought to herself as she started up that steep high street and stopped in a fairly cheap clothes shop, the things you needed that you never really thought about. Underwear. Pyjamas. Toothpaste. Clean clothes. A hairbrush. Things that were normally just to hand - and yet now she had to buy from scratch, because she'd left it all behind. It almost seemed wasteful, really, to buy these new things for one night - but this was the second night she'd been away from home, and she couldn't cope any longer. Besides - it wasn't as though she didn't have the savings.

After treating herself to some delicious smelling fudge from a shop where you could see it being made in the window, and the essential shopping trip, Lee decided to call it a night and have some dinner. It was emotionally draining keeping that large raincloud from over her head; avoiding that one topic from pervading her thoughts.

It was probably the earliest she had eaten dinner in years - and the first time she could remember eating dinner out alone. Even though it was only half past five, it was pitch black outside and the small restaurant had candles lit at every table. Lee waited until after she'd ordered to face the music and see the message she had been shielding herself from all day.

Two texts from Beth - she could cope with those.

You left without saying goodbye! Hope you're okay. X

Lee, mum knows you're not at home - please let her (and me!) know you're okay to save my sanity. X

Ah, Lee thought. Perhaps Nathan had been in touch with mum? Or maybe mum had phoned home. She presumed at least one of the five voicemails was from her mother - but she couldn't face them just yet. Instead she sent a joint text to both Beth and her mum.

I'm fine - spending a night in Devon. Not too specific, she thought - nothing that could get back to Nathan. *Ring soon. L x*

The next text was from Tania.

Feeling any better? X

Now that, unfortunately, needed to be dealt with directly. She thought the best way was to be honest because - to be totally truthful, she didn't think she could face going in tomorrow or the day after. In fact, right now she felt a little shaky, felt as though something was buzzing in her head. She felt as though if she went back to her everyday life she would simply cry. Or scream. Or possibly both. And she needed to feel in control of that before she stepped foot back in the office.

I'm really sorry, but I need the week off, she wrote, copying in both Tania and Gemma. She knew it would provoke phone calls; she also knew she couldn't face answering them. *I walked in on Nathan cheating on me and I need to get my head together. Speak soon. Lee x*

As she hit send, she couldn't believe she had really put it into words. It felt so real… so final.

But it was real. And it was final. Furiously rubbing away the tears that were falling from her eyes, she knew that was something she needed to accept.

Change was just so damn hard.

CHAPTER FIVE

Despite the much-needed nap, Lee didn't find it hard to sleep that night. After a nice solo meal - in which she ignored the messages building up on her phone and instead started a second hand mystery novel she'd picked up in the charity shop - Lee had treated herself to a large glass of wine from the pub she was staying above, had a soak in the bath, changed into her brand new, clean pyjamas and snuggled in to watch some television.

It had been a while since she'd sat and watched television without having some plan of what she was watching. She and Nathan had been so busy that if there was anything they wanted to watch it needed to be planned in - recorded or watched on demand; very, very rarely when it was originally broadcast. But now she found herself with the most elusive of things: time. Something she hadn't had the luxury of for a long time - and which she was going to take advantage of now. She had this night - and then she would need to drive back to Bristol, find somewhere new to live, look into a divorce, start her whole life afresh.

For now, however, she enjoyed mindlessly watching whatever came on the television. The large glass of white wine had a soporific effect, and along with the slightly monotonous voice of the presenter on whatever TV show it was she was watching, it wasn't long before she was lulled into the most peaceful and dreamless sleep she'd had in a long time.

* * *

Breakfast, she decided (having put on the new clothes she had bought yesterday and packed up her few meagre belongings, ready for check out at 1pm) had to be at the little café she had eaten at the day before. The food had been delicious, and she could people watch as much as she wanted from that little table in the window.

"Good morning dear!" It was the same woman who had served Lee the day before, and she obviously recognised the repeat customer. "Are you new to the area?"

Lee smiled; "Only visiting, I'm afraid. It's lovely here, isn't it!"

"Oh, I wouldn't live anywhere else than Totnes," the grey haired lady told her, passing her a menu and setting out some cutlery. "It's got its quirks, that's for sure, but I've never felt more at home anywhere. Now, dear, can I get you some tea?"

"Yes, thanks." Lee watched a young family come in and take a seat as she perused the menu; mum, dad, young boy and baby girl. She had to look away; the scene made her heart ache a little. Something that had seemed on the horizon; something that had been pushed even further into the distance.

She had wasted the best years of her life on Nathan; and now he'd screwed her over royally.

"How long have you worked here?" she asked the waitress conversationally as she took her order.

"Worked here, and run the place, for ten years. All coming to an end soon though - I'm retiring you see. I'm leaving next month, presuming I can find someone to take the lease. That's why everyone's out there protesting - there's been a lot of interest from a massive coffee chain. Not the sort of thing we want here, really - we like to keep it local." There was a slightly pained look on her face. "I don't want to sell them the lease but… I'm getting on a bit, if truth be told, my hips aren't what they used to be and I just can't keep working the hours I am."

Lee felt for her; she was clearly torn between loyalty and her need for a bit of rest and relaxation.

The conversation continued to play on her mind as she ate her full English breakfast, and as she wandered up the steep high street, getting her steps in for the day and perusing the weekly market stalls. She saw beautiful carved wooden spoons that she thought would go perfectly in her marble kitchen - and then promptly remembered that it wasn't her kitchen anymore. Even if she got him out of the house, she didn't think she could ever feel the same about it again - not after seeing him in their bed with that woman…

She passed a brightly coloured scarf - black with multi coloured paint splats printed all over it - which caught her eye. Immediately she moved on, thinking how strange it was that she'd even stopped - it was so not *her*. And then she thought: What is me? Promptly, she turned round and bought the scarf, deciding to make it the beginning of whatever leaf she was turning over.

And that really would have been it: a new scarf, a few new cheap clothes and an impromptu night away in Totnes. It would have been, had she not seen the sign that would change at least the next few weeks of her life in the most strange and wonderful ways.

Flatmate wanted IMMEDIATELY due to let down and rent needing paying! Laid back twenty-something female, fairly neat and tidy, fan of early nights and cups of tea. One well behaved (usually!) cat, five minute walk into town. Call Totnes 554321. Gina

It spoke to Lee like nothing she had ever read before. This Gina sounded so informal, so free and easy - and she needed someone to live with her. And Lee needed somewhere to live. Never mind that she worked in Bristol, never mind that she had a life and a shambles of a marriage and a mother and a sister that she needed to go and deal with. Lee Jones, for one of the first times in her life, threw caution to the wind and made a truly spontaneous and more than slightly crazy decision. She found the dialling code for Totnes, and she dialled that number…

CHAPTER SIX

It had all happened in rather a whirlwind. After ringing Gina and finding out the room was still available, she went to see it and to meet this Gina (to make sure she wasn't some kind of axe murderer, and vice versa she presumed.) Gina was a couple of years younger than Lee, with red hair that looked too bright to be wholly natural and a nose ring. She was as laid back as Lee had thought she sounded - as was the flat. The room for rent was fairly plain, although it did have a double bed and wardrobe in it. The rest of the flat was decorated in brighter colours, with beaded curtains hanging in every door and brightly coloured throws on the sofa and arm chair. The mostly well behaved cat sat curled up on the arm of the sofa, and purred happily when Lee stroked it.

It was so different than anywhere Lee had ever lived; it had so much personality. She immediately loved it.

"When can you move in?" Gina asked, ten minutes after meeting her; she had obviously passed whatever test meeting her had provided.

A little nervously, Lee bit her fingernails on her left hand and tried to work out what on earth her plan was. She guessed there hadn't really been a plan; she'd seen the sign, rung, come round - and here she was. Was she really going to stay in this little town for any length of time? What about work?

Work, she had reasoned on the way over, could actually wait. She wanted to make herself happy for once - and this little town made her happy, or so it seemed. She could take a sabbatical for a few weeks…

"Tonight?" Lee asked with a hopeful grin.

"Yeah, sure!" If Gina was surprised, she didn't say anything.

"I have to be honest though - I don't know if I'll be here longer than a month. I can pay you a month's rent up front though..."

"Done," Gina said. "Just let me know so I can find someone to take the room if you're leaving, yeah?" It was all so easy - keys were handed over, Gina went off to do her shift in a local restaurant, and Lee found herself alone in a room that was now hers - needing to collect her stuff from the hotel and tell her nearest and dearest that she'd decided to stay two hours away for the foreseeable future.

It didn't take long to transfer her few belongings from the hotel to the flat right at the top of the town, especially once she'd collected her car from the car park and paid the hotel bill. The harder job came once she'd returned to the new bedroom (with a quick stop at the local supermarket for towels and bedding); time to let people know that she'd decided to take an extended break in the South West. And she didn't think a text or email was going to cut it this time.

Taking a deep breath, she dialled the office and heard Tania's voice after a few rings.

"Hello, Phillips, Jones and Sharpe, Tania Sharpe speaking."

"Hi, Tania - it's Lee."

"Lee! We were so worried about you when you messaged. And then you haven't replied since! Are you okay? Nathan is a wanker - I cannot believe he's done that to you."

When she was able to get a word in edgeways, Lee replied: "Thanks, Tan. I'm okay, I think. As okay as you can expect when you walk in on your husband naked with another woman."

"I can't believe it... I'm so sorry. He's been in here, you know, looking for you."

"Oh?" Lee didn't know if she was interested or not; surprised or not. She felt nothing.

"Yeah, in a bit of a state, said you weren't answering your phone."

"Certainly not to him," Lee said darkly.

"Don't blame you. And we told him nothing, so don't worry - and Gemma had a few choice words for him. He left with his tail between his legs, I'll tell you that."

"Thanks. Anyway, I need to talk with you - and Gemma."

"Can you say it tomorrow? I think she's with a client at the minute."

"No, I can't Tania - can you see if she's free?"

There was silence on the other end of the phone for a few moments, and Lee took the opportunity to have a wander round the flat. A small kitchen with a dining table; a bathroom with a bath and shower, and dolphins tiled into the walls; and the two bedrooms.

"Lee?" Gemma's voice now - she could tell it was on speaker by the slightly fuzzy quality to their voices.

"Hi Gemma."

"What a bastard, Lee - and I told him that, believe me. I'm so sorry."

“Thank you - both of you, I appreciate it. The thing is - I’ve decided to take some leave from work. I know it’s not fair on you both, and I’m sorry, and I know I should really give more notice - but I had no idea this was going to happen. And I just need some time…”

Again there was silence on the other end of the line; Lee could picture them looking at each other in horror. Or maybe just confusion…

“Okay… how long for?”

“A few weeks? I need to do this - need some time out of everything while I make some decisions. I’m going to stay in Devon.”

“In Devon? Lee," Tania asked, blunt as ever. "Are you having a mental breakdown?"

"I don't know," Lee said truthfully. "I feel okay. I just need to do this.”

The phone call ended a little awkwardly, but they both wished her well and promised they would hold down the fort for as long as she needed, provided she let them know how she was getting on. They also promised not to tell Nathan a thing.

She thought her sister might take it a little better than her colleagues; after all, Beth had always been a free spirit who had chosen her own path in life. Lee settled down on the sofa with a cup of tea (she had to borrow milk, tea and a mug from Gina, and made a mental note to go and buy some groceries later that evening) for a long chat with her sister - enjoying the prospect of another work free day in the morning.

*   *   *

After a marathon phone call with her sister - who had also questioned her sanity, and had also had contact from Nathan - Lee had driven to the nearest supermarket to stock up on essentials for the kitchen and the bedroom, before settling down for an early night.

When she got up the next morning, she almost didn't recognise her surroundings; life had moved so quickly in the last few days that she felt her brain couldn't really catch up. She was a little surprised - although she wasn't really sure why - to find Gina sat in her pyjamas in the living room.

"Morning," Gina said, glancing over as Lee walked in before turning back to her novel. Lee didn't think she could remember the last time she'd lived with someone she wasn't romantically involved with: probably not since university.

After making a cup of coffee, Lee padded across the carpeted living room floor and sat on the armchair opposite Gina.

"So," Gina said, looking at Lee over her large mug of tea. "What do you do?"

"Me? Oh, I'm a lawyer."

"A lawyer? What are you doing in a flat share?"

"It's a long story…" Lee fiddled with the fringing around the throw she was sat on.

"I've got nowhere to be!" Gina said with a grin. "Besides, if we're going to live together we should probably know a little more about each other than just our first names…"

The Lee of last week would have probably thought someone living with a person when they only knew their first name was certifiably insane - but she found that it didn't really worry her now. She had a good feeling about Gina - and so the events of the last few days began to pour out.

"So you've only been in Totnes two days? And you don't have a job?"

"Well, I do have a job, but no, I'm not working it at the minute. And yes - two days."

"Wow. And I thought I was impulsive… still, guess it makes you think, finding out the man you chose to marry is a total and utter shit." She covered her mouth with her hand and her eyes widened slightly. "Oops, sorry. Don't mean to be an insensitive bitch - I'm a bit blunt, or so my friends tell me."

Lee laughed - and was a little surprised to find that it wasn't forced or fake. "No, he is a shit. And it has turned my life upside down…"

"Why here?"

"I don't honestly know," Lee admitted. "I drove, and I got here and… well, it's got a certain vibe, hasn't it?"

"The lingering smell of pot, most people refer to it as!" Gina said with a smirk. "No, I kid - Totnes has something special, everyone says so. That's why our high street is always heaving and people are desperate to live here!"

"And now…" Lee sighed and sipped her coffee, trying to find the words. "I just couldn't face going back to my ordinary life, you know? Without…him, without everything I thought my life was going to be…" Why she was pouring her heart out to a virtual stranger - one she happened to be living with, but that was beside the point - she wasn't sure, but it felt good to voice it.

"Sometimes we sleepwalk through life, I think," Gina said. "And it takes something like this to wake us up and take stock of what we really want in life. Stay as long as you want, Lee - I have a feeling we'll get on just fine. As long as you can pay the rent!"

"Already in your bank account," Lee said with a smile. "Thanks, Gina. I think Totnes might be just what I need."

"As I'm guessing you don't know anyone, and you don't have a job here or anything, do you want to come out with a few of us this evening?"

"I don't want to intrude…" Lee said, feeling like the invite sounded very much like it was done out of pity.

"No, that came out wrong - I just meant that since I now know you might actually want to hang out with a bunch of strangers, you'd be more than welcome. They're turning on the Christmas lights - it's quite the event! Mulled wine, the town crier - all the fun of small town living. Go on, I won't take no for an answer."

Lee weighed up the options in her mind for a moment - a night in alone or a festive evening with new people.

"Okay - I'll come," she said, plumping for the second option. She hoped it might rekindle her Christmas spirit that had been somewhat dampened by recent events.

* * *

She chose a black laced top and a pair of black jeans from her limited clothing collection, and paired it with black boots that she'd picked up in a charity shop. It wasn't that money was tight - she had enough savings to keep her going past the month she said she'd be away - but they'd been in good condition and she'd thought it was better to give money to a good cause than buy another pair of new shoes to add to the many pairs in her Bristol wardrobe.

At the top of the town, where the market had been the previous day, she met Gina and her three friends - Dan, Kelly and Lydia. They were all a couple of years younger than Lee, but accepted her onto their evening out readily. If Gina had shared the details of her appearance in Totnes, they didn't let on, for which she was glad; they also didn't ask her many personal questions, which made life much simpler.

In the centre of the square stood a massive green Christmas tree, majestic in both height and decoration. There wasn't really a unifying colour - instead ornaments and baubles in red, green, silver and blue were sprinkled throughout the tree, all leading up to a large star that was so glittery it sparkled in just the moonlight. Lights were strung around the tree although they could barely be seen - of course they had not yet been turned on. Christmas market stalls had been erected but weren't yet open; the signs told Lee that they would open on the first of December - two more weeks. Lee found herself feeling happy that she would still be around to see it; she thought it might be quite a festive experience.

"Lee?" The sound of her name broke her reverie, and she turned to find Gina looking at her with a slightly bemused experience.

"Sorry, in my own little world. What did you say?"

"Do you want mulled wine? We're all getting some."

"Sounds lovely, thanks."

They toasted the Christmas tree - apparently one of Gina's Christmas traditions - and found a good spot to huddle before the lights were officially turned on.

"Hear ye, hear ye, on the sixteenth of November, these Christmas lights will be lit. Hear ye, hear ye, gather round for the start of the Christmas season!" The town crier, dressed in old fashioned clothing and a large hat, walked the streets, ringing his bell and announcing the event to come. Lee found herself trying not to laugh; she wasn't sure she'd ever seen anything like it before.

With five minutes to go, a large group of carollers - mixed in age from around 9 to 90 - gathered in front of the tree and pulled out red folders. Together they began to sing traditional carols, and Lee felt a little shiver travel down her spine, despite the surprisingly mild evening. The Christmas magic felt particularly strong tonight.

Quite a large crowd had gathered by the time the local mayor stood in front of the tree with a big red button, ready to turn on the lights.

"Five, four, three…" Everyone chanted the count down, and at zero the mayor pressed the button and looked relieved when everything went to plan. Hundreds of tiny blue and white lights flickered to life, looking like tiny fairies nestled in the branches of the beautiful fir. At the same time, lights strung across from one side of the high street to the other flashed on; a mixture of festive tableaus and words announcing 'Merry Christmas' and 'Welcome to Totnes'.

The group listened to the carollers for another ten minutes or so, by which time the crowd had started to disperse.

"Shall we go and get a proper drink?" Lydia asked as they finished their mulled wine.

"Sounds like a plan. What about dinner? I've not eaten yet."

"The vegetarian restaurant's only a few doors away..." Dan said, hopefully.

"Oh, Dan!" Kelly said. "You always want to go to the bloody vegetarian restaurant!"

"The food's great," Dan said, stuffing his hands in his pockets.

"If you're vegetarian - which is only you. Oh, sorry, Lee, are you?" Gina said.

"No, afraid not!"

"There," Gina responded with one hand on her hip, nose ring glinting in the Christmas lights. "One vegetarian cannot decide for the other four. Anyway, we're going there next week for a meal, aren't we - so tonight let's do pizza. Always good vegetarian options at a pizza place."

With only a slight grumble from Dan, the five set off up the hill, chatting companionably about not very much at all.

CHAPTER SEVEN

Lee had been living in Totnes for six days before she made it back to the little café that she had first eaten in on the day she'd arrived. She had still not made any contact with Nathan, although she had endured a rather painful conversation with her mother who had asked what on Earth she was doing in the middle of nowhere and whether her marriage truly was over.

Lee had assured her that her marriage was most certainly over, and that she was getting her head together in the middle of nowhere. And it seemed to be working; it was getting slightly less painful to think of Nathan each day. Painful, but not that soul ripping pain she had endured on the day she'd walked in on them. Perhaps it was just time; perhaps it was being away from everything. She didn't want to go back and find out which it was.

She went into the café for lunch this time, and was served once again by Val.

"Hello dear!" she exclaimed as soon as the door closed behind Lee. "And here I thought you were only here for a night and would never return!"

"Well," Lee said with a smile. "I have a confession - that was the plan. But I couldn't leave… so I've decided to stay for the foreseeable future. There's something about this place…"

"Oh that's certainly true! I came here in 1972, planning to only be here a few months before moving on - and here I still am!"

"Any luck with selling your lease?" Lee asked as she ordered jacket potato for her lunch.

She regretted the words once they had left her mouth; Val's face fell and she shook her head sadly. "There's been some interest, but no-one seems to be ready to part with the money - no-one except massive corporations that I know the town just won't accept."

"I'm sorry," Lee said truthfully. "I wish I could help."

"Thank you dear. You enjoy your lunch, don't worry about me. I'm glad you'll be sticking around for a while longer - always nice to see fresh faces!"

As she ate her lunch, Lee mulled over Val's problem. She had no idea how much a lease cost, no idea how she could help such a kind, friendly woman. She enjoyed the same seat again, watching the world go by outside the window for a long time after her plate had been cleared away, letting her thoughts take over her mind…

* * *

She enjoyed a slow walk back up the hill, popping into shops and picking up another couple of second hand novels from the charity shop. As much as she was enjoying the slower pace of life, there was a niggling thought at the back of her head; what was she going to do with her time if she stayed here for a month? She had rarely taken more than a few days off work, and that was usually when they were going somewhere abroad on holiday. She hadn't had time at home to just *be* for a long time - possibly not since she'd been at uni.

As Gina was working lunch today, she planned to get home and spend an hour or so reading, before perhaps doing some housework. Although she was paying rent, she still felt a little odd about living in someone's home, and thought it would be nice to help out a bit and make things a little easier for Gina. Besides, it would give her something to do.

She was only ten minutes into her novel and cup of tea combo when the door burst open and an irritated looking Gina walked in.

"They cut my hours back to nothing," Gina said, looking miserable. "I don't know what I'm going to do." She threw herself onto the brightly coloured sofa, sighing deeply, and looked at Lee. "I've worked there for the last two years on and off and now they haven't got enough hours for me. Right before Christmas too. It sucks. I don't know how I'm going to pay the rent, especially not if you leave…"

"How can they do that? That doesn't seem fair." The lawyer in Lee began to get angry. "Let me look at your contract; I'm sure there's something we can do." Gina smiled a half smile. "It's a zero hours contract," she said, shrugging. "There's nothing I can do - they haven't actually sacked me, there just aren't any hours - zero hours in fact."

"It is terrible timing," Lee said. "I'm so sorry."

Lee's mind began to whir at this point, thinking through all the things that happened in the day and how they could possibly - just possibly - come together. Somehow she thought she had fallen in love with that little café at the bottom of the town and she couldn't bear the thought of it being turned into something else - or some massive corporation that would be so out of place in this idyllic little town getting its hands on it. And she certainly could not just stay at home and do nothing for four weeks - or maybe longer; who knew what would happen? When she did leave, maybe there was a way to leave part of her in this town. Hopefully not the only happy part of her…

"I've got an idea," Lee said with a glint in her eye and a smile on her lips. "Something I think might be good for both of us - and maybe a few other people round here."

Gina was immediately intrigued: "Go on," she said.

“I need to check a few things out first,” Lee said. “I don't want to get anyone's hopes up if it's not possible. But don't lose faith just yet - maybe we can have a little Christmas miracle of our own!”

* * *

Lee considered waiting until the next day, but the idea was buzzing around the back of her head, making her think of nothing else. She drove this time, as the weather had turned wet and dark and she had a plan to drive to Dartmouth that evening, to see if it was anything like she remembered.

She managed to park almost outside the café, dusting off the parallel parking skills she had not regularly used in many years, and was so excited she almost bounced into the coffee shop.

“How does one buy a lease?” she asked Val the second the door had closed. No-one else was there; Val was slowly packing up, ready to head home. Her last customer had left five minutes previously.

“Oh, hello again. Sorry, to buy a lease?”

“Yes. How much is it, and what does someone have to do to buy it?”

Val looked confused at the turn of the conversation, but duly shuffled in a pile of paperwork beneath the till and pulled out the information needed. “It’s all in there - the prices, the process, how it all works. But why do you need to know?”

Lee didn’t speak for a few moments, flicking through the documents in front of her. She was pleased then for her lawyer training - she could understand everything written and could tell that the paperwork wasn’t signing over anything crazy. It was a ten year lease - although it could be sold on, of course, if a willing buyer was found - and the cost was certainly doable; presuming it could turn some sort of a profit.

"I hate to ask, Val - but what sort of profit are you making?" A little more shuffling and another pile of paperwork was produced.

"It's all there - I've got nothing to hide. The accountant keeps an eye on it all too. You will have to explain the interrogation in a minute though, young lady!" She spoke with a smile, and Lee smiled back before pulling up a stool and perusing the paperwork. After a few minutes, Val started her tidying up again, occasionally throwing bemused glances at this whirlwind of a woman who had come in and asked to see her financial paperwork.

The smile didn't leave Lee's face as she leafed through the paperwork. It certainly wasn't making millions, but it did turn a small profit. A profit that could perhaps be capitalised on, if someone knew what they were doing in a busy high street like this... Not that Lee did know what she was doing. But she thought she knew someone who might; and she thought she could learn.

"Okay," she finally said, piling the paperwork up and handing it back to Val. "I'd like to buy the lease."

"You want to buy the lease?" There was a look of shock and disbelief in Val's lined features. Then her eyes narrowed. "I thought you were only going to be here for a month."

"I probably am. Maybe longer. But I love this place - and I have a plan. I can buy the lease, I can get it all started and then - not that I've asked her yet - I think I can persuade my flatmate to take over the running of it if - when - I leave. Do you know her? Gina Travis."

"Oh, everyone round here knows Gina. Used to be a bit of a madam back in the day, getting into trouble, but she's settled down a lot since then. Besides, I never minded a bit of graffiti myself..."

She was clearly mulling things over, and Lee let that new piece of information sink in as she waited for a response.

"It all seems a little sudden, dear. You turn up, you decide to stay, you want to buy the lease to a café..."

"I've never been a spontaneous person in my life, Val. I'm a lawyer. I've got a solid career, I have - I had, a marriage and a nice house. And this week I've made more spontaneous decisions than in the last five years - and I feel alive. I *want* to do this. I can afford to do this. You don't need to feel like you're taking advantage of me - I promise. Just say yes..."

Val only paused for a moment; "Yes!" she said, and a broad grin spread across her face, making the wrinkles seem less obvious and her eyes seem brighter. The tiredness seemed to lift from her as she reached across the counter and gave Lee a hug. "I'll get in touch with my lawyer in the morning. You've made me a very happy woman, Lee... What is your last name?"

"Lee Jones," she immediately said - and found the sound of it didn't sit well in her mouth. "Actually no - I'm not keeping his surname, not when he decided to ruin our marriage. Lee Davis. Back to my maiden name - that's the way forward."

"Well," Val said, putting her small hand over Lee's. "His loss is very definitely our gain."

* * *

She drove straight from the café to the small town of Dartmouth where she had visited a few years previously on holiday. Luckily it was somewhere she had been with her mum and sister, not Nathan; she wanted to avoid anywhere with memories of Nathan right now. She knew there had been good times, but she didn't see the need to look back on their marriage with any lens of positivity right now; there was far too much anger and far too much hurt.

She still hadn't answered his phone calls, which had dropped off a little - only two today, although she'd set her phone to automatically reject them. As she drove along the windy country roads, surrounded by hedgerows as the stars and moon lit up the sky above her, Lee played Christmas tunes through the car speakers. That Christmas magic still felt alive, she was pleased to find - even with her current state of mind. The four weeks she'd said she would stay would take her to the twentieth of December - but she found herself imagining herself in that little flat for Christmas day and thought it wasn't a terrible idea. She planned to give it another week and see how she felt then; she certainly thought that the Christmas magic felt stronger here than it had back in Bristol.

Despite the dark and the rain, Lee recognised Dartmouth before her sat nav told her she'd arrived. Christmas lights were strung up here too; multi coloured light bulbs that lit up the water and the rain and made the whole place feel like it was some sort of dream. Wrapping up in the raincoat she'd found in her latest charity shop trip (which was two sizes too big but didn't seem to let any water in) and an umbrella she'd found languishing in the boot of the car, Lee battled her way over to the railings and stood overlooking the water. In the distance she could see the lights of a boat; in the water the Christmas lights on the railings and in the trees were reflected, twinkling like lost sailors in the water. She wasn't sure how long she stood there for, but the rain hitting her face made her feel something - something strong, something very much like being alive. It felt like Gina had been right when she'd said about sleepwalking through life…

When she realised she had begun to shiver - and that passers-by probably thought she was crazy, staring over at brightly coloured houses that she only *knew* were brightly coloured from a photo she had on her desk at work - she decided to head back to the car. Her eye was caught by the warm, inviting, yellow lights of a large hotel; at the same time her stomach rumbled.

It was an old fashioned hotel, with a black and white facade and a large restaurant with golden chandeliers. It was the fanciest place she had ever eaten alone, and let alone as soaking wet as she was, but she bravely asked for a table for one and was seated in a window seat looking out into the bleak rain, punctuated every so often by Christmas lights. Window seats seemed to have become her thing; watching other people living their lives as she tried to figure out the direction in which hers was going.

Once she'd ordered from a waiter who she was sure was judging her dishevelled, wet appearance, she pulled out her phone and fired a text off to Gina. *Plan in motion. I'll be home by 9, talk then if you're up!* Gina responded with a smiley face and a thumbs up.

It was with her phone open and no dining companion that she made the questionable decision to read the unread messages in her inbox. Almost all of them were from Nathan and, without really knowing what she was doing, she clicked 'open' and began to read the one-sided conversation.

Lee, I'm so sorry. Please ring me - N.

Lee - where are you? You haven't been home and I'm worried. N x

Your sister says you're in Devon - I don't understand. We need to talk about this - I can't fix it if we don't talk. Nathan x

Our marriage isn't over, Lee, it can't be - ring me, we can work through this. N xx

This is ridiculous. I think you're being childish to just ignore me. Nathan.

I'm sorry, I shouldn't have said that. I've spoken to your mum and we're worried about you - ring me Lee, please. For our marriage. Nathan x

Her emotions cycled through many phases as she read them, from nostalgic, to upset, to furious. She settled on angry. How dare he say she was childish? How dare he say he was worried? It was his decisions, his actions, his inability to control his penis that had led them here - she'd not cheated, not even considered it. She'd not taken some colleague back to their marital bed and…and…

She felt tears, hot and furious, running down her cheeks and tried to wipe them away before she added to the crazy 'staring into the darkness in the rain' image that she had already propagated with the people of Dartmouth.

She felt somehow that the people in Totnes wouldn't have thought she was quite as strange.

CHAPTER EIGHT

Gina was waiting up when she walked in, and she was pleased that she had got control over her emotions before seeing her new friend and flatmate.

"You look like you got soaked," Gina commented, sat in her pyjamas under another of the brightly coloured throws that seemed to multiply around the flat.

"Oh, I definitely did. Blew away the cobwebs though! Let me stick the kettle on and get out of these wet clothes and then I'll tell you everything..."

"Hurry up then!" Gina shouted as Lee went into her bedroom. "You've had me on tenterhooks all evening!" Lee laughed but insisted on making a cup of tea before she spilled the beans.

"Okay. You're probably going to think I'm mad-"

"That ship sailed when you randomly turned up in Totnes with no clothes, nowhere to live and no job I'm afraid," Gina said with a smirk.

"Oh, okay, fair enough, even more mad. But I've got a great plan."

And so she told her - told her about the café, the lease, her dreams for it and how she hoped that Gina would run it once she'd left.

"Let me get this straight. You'd be paying the lease, you'd be paying me for working there, and I'd be in charge once you were gone?"

"Yeah, that's the plan, if you're interested..." Suddenly she wasn't so convinced by her plan - what if Gina didn't want that sort of responsibility? Then she'd have to find someone else she could trust as the manager once she'd left town - and she wasn't sure why, but she felt an easy trust with Gina that she thought might be hard to replicate.

"Of course I'm bloody interested! That sorts my job problem and Val's lease problem in one fell swoop. I just don't really get what's in it for you - not that I'm criticising!"

Lee sighed. "I guess… There's just something about that place. And I can't sit here and do nothing - wallowing in my sadness and self-pity won't help me. I need to do something, something to wipe away all the rubbish so when I go back, I go back with a fresh slate, ready to start again. And this came up and I thought… why not! So she's speaking to her lawyers tomorrow, and hopefully we can get in there pretty soon! I've got some menu ideas and some redecorating ideas…"

They spent a companionable evening discussing colour schemes, menu choices, names and ways to get the customers through the doors - and by the time Lee went to bed she felt a lot more confident in her spontaneous decision. She truly felt they could make this a success.

* * *

As the nights got colder and the end of November was in sight, Lee found that the café plan went far more smoothly than she could have possibly imagined. Val was keen to begin her retirement; Lee didn't need to hire a lawyer and had plenty of savings. One thing she was eminently grateful for now was that she had always kept her savings in her account from before she was married, and continued to pay into it. While she was still using their join account for every day expenses, she could take large deposits from her own savings account without anyone batting an eye lid. Soon, she knew, she should try to discuss the financial situation with Nathan - but it wasn't something she could face just yet.

Once the lease had been signed and the keys had been handed over, Lee immediately closed the café in order to get things sorted. She was so excited when she wrote the sign that she had to stop several times as her hand was shaking. *Under new management! Closed for refurbishment. Reopening December 1st.*

December first - it was perfect. The build up to Christmas, the market, the countdown, the excitement… That would get people through the doors, she was sure of it.

On the first day after they closed, she and Gina headed down in their oldest clothes, hair scraped back and tins of paint at the ready. It was only a small space; eight tables, the counter and a small room out the back. It needed a decent spruce up, and they'd decided on a whole new colour scheme together: grey baseboards and counters, with duck egg blue for the walls. They threw themselves into the task whole heartedly, covering the coffee machine and the tables with old sheets, getting ladders and playing music from Gina's radio that she'd brought along. At the end of the first day they were paint-splattered, exhausted, but happy with their progress.

On the second day they painted another coat, and stood high up on ladders to paint blackboard paint way up behind the coffee machine; by late afternoon they were building a new tall table with help from Gina's friends Dan, Kelly and Lydia. Along with high stools that Lee had ordered online, she hoped that they would be busy enough to need the extra seating.

"It's looking great in here Lee - a real breath of fresh air," Dan said as he drilled into the wall.

"Yeah, we've told everyone to make sure they get down here December first - you should be packed!" Kelly added. She was holding the new counter up while Lydia used the spirit level to make sure coffees weren't going to go whizzing off the table as soon as someone put them down.

"Thank you - and thanks again for coming in. We couldn't have got all this done alone!"

"It's fine - I'm sure you'll make it up to us in coffees!"

Gina laughed. "Discount maybe, but no mates rates. Right, Lee, I'll get started on the sign for out front shall I? Dad dropped off the piece of wood, it looks great - now I've just got to make sure the lettering stands up to scrutiny!"

"Your calligraphy is brilliant, Gina, I have every faith." That had been another lucky coincidence - when tidying up around the flat the previous week, Lee had stumbled across pages of beautiful letters - band names, people's names, sayings, you name it - and had discovered that Gina was the artist behind it. So of course she had to paint the sign for their new business venture.

It was an exceptionally busy week, with stock to be ordered, adverts to be put in papers and shop windows, painting to finish and cleaning to do. On the Friday night, just a weekend between them and the opening day, Lee and Gina sat in their paint splattered garments on the floor of the café with a bottle of wine and two glasses.

"Here's to our new venture," Gina said, raising her glass to toast Lee. "And to friendship. And to Totnes!" It wasn't the first glass of wine they'd had, and Lee giggled and toasted back each time.

"I'm so pleased, Gina. It looks better than I could ever have imagined." She gestured to the space around her; the menu written up on the blackboard paint behind them (in Gina's beautiful handwriting, of course) listing every kind of coffee imaginable. Soya milk, nut milk, goats' milk - and cows' milk too, of course.

Food had left the menu for now, but they planned to cater for every coffee and cake need they could. Dairy free cakes, gluten free cakes, different sponges and cookies and fruit cakes… all locally sourced or made in house. Gina had proven to be a real find; not only did she hold food hygiene qualifications, she'd also had experience making all these weird and wonderful hot drinks that they had dreamed up together. It was a partnership made in heaven.

In the far left corner of the menu was Lee's favourite part, and the part she had had been personally responsible for. On a blackboard surrounded by drawings of holly and tinsel was a menu of 'festive favourites'; gingerbread hot chocolates, mint lattes, mistletoe and raspberry tea… the list went on, a list of drinks and cakes that brought some of the Christmas magic that Lee often felt into the forefront of their little café.

"Come on. Let's lock up and get home - we'll need to get our sleep before the craziness of opening a new business really hits us!" They downed the ends of their glasses of wine, leaving the glasses next to the dishwasher and the bottle in the recycling bin, then exited the premises. After locking up, they linked arms, ready to start the long walk up the hill and through the town to their little home.

"Lee." The voice came from the darkness behind them, and they both stopped their tipsy giggling to turn and see who it was.

When Lee saw, the alcohol and cheer seemed to evaporate from her veins in a heartbeat.

"How… how did you find me?"

"Our bank account statements. You'd been spending regular amounts in this café, so I looked it up…"

Lee didn't explain that she owned the business now; she didn't explain the paint splattered clothing, nor introduce her new friend.

"We need to talk, Lee."

"Is this him?" Gina asked, and Lee nodded.

"Nathan," Lee said, his name feeling strange as it passed her lips for the first time in a couple of weeks. "There's nothing to say."

"Nothing to say? You upped and left, we haven't discussed anything. We're married, Lee, that means something to me."

Lee laughed. It was a slightly manic laugh, but it was laughter all the same. "It means something to you? It means something to you? You cheated, Nathan. You slept with those two women - and maybe more, I don't know. Our marriage meant nothing to you, clearly - and now it means nothing to me. Leave me alone."

Nathan took a step towards her, his eyes sparkling a little in the moonlight, his hair falling haphazardly across the dark skin of his forehead.

"Do you want me to go?" Gina asked, and Lee was torn; part of her didn't want to be alone with him, while the other part didn't want to make a fool of herself in front of someone whose good opinion she wanted.

"Do you mind starting to walk up the hill? I'll be right behind you, I just need to get rid of him."

Gina nodded, and fixed Nathan with a stare full of hatred, before turning on her heel and beginning to meander up the hill.

"Lee," Nathan said again, his voice softening. He took another step towards her and reached for her hand; Lee recoiled at his touch. She looked up at him and their eyes met; she fixed him with a steely glare and took a deep breath before addressing him.

“Don’t touch me. You destroyed everything we ever had.” She swallowed, but pushed on before he had a chance to interrupt her. “I want a divorce.” She couldn’t quite believe the words were out of her mouth; she hadn’t planned it, she was just so angered by his words that it came out. But it wasn’t just her anger that fuelled her words; she meant them, she was sure of it. She looked him in the eye and could not even think what she saw in him. His actions had destroyed her feelings for him, but also her respect; he had hurt her so cruelly she could not even consider her life with him in it.

He was in shock, she thought; he certainly stood there for a few minutes, his mouth slightly agape, no words coming out.

And then Lee turned on her heel and marched up the hill of Totnes high street, beneath the strings of Christmas lights, ignoring the shouts of ‘Lee’ once Nathan finally found his voice.

CHAPTER NINE

Pleased that Nathan didn't know her address, she enjoyed a hot shower to remove the paint and dust from her body before snuggling down into her bed with a freshly made hot water bottle. Sleep eluded her for a long time, despite the multiple glasses of wine, as she replayed the evening's events in her head. She hadn't expected to see him; he seemed so out of place there, stood on the street outside her little café, that she had been in shock for a while.

It was his words, though, that haunted her. Why wasn't he more repentant? Why wasn't he begging for forgiveness? She just didn't understand. He said he was sorry, yes - but he wasn't flooded with remorse. He gave excuses, he blamed her for leaving, he made statements that made no sense… If he really wanted their marriage, if it really had been a stupid mistake, wouldn't he be devastated?

She wondered whether he really wanted to fight for their marriage at all, or whether he was just going through the motions, doing what was expected of him.

Would he stay the night somewhere, or would he drive straight back? She didn't like how much he was on her mind this evening; what had been such an enjoyable evening had been soured by his appearance. Gina had realised she didn't want to talk about it, and had kept her questions to a minimum - and yet here Lee was, with his name and his words running round her head, making the sleep that had come so easily in recent days elusive.

It was late when she fell into a fitful sleep, with twisted dreams filling her mind. Images of Nathan, of the blonde, an imagined image of the nurse he'd spoken of at work… they all melded into one nightmare, held in their bedroom back in Bristol. Brandon, the sexist pig who'd overturned her for a male lawyer, appeared there too, although it made no sense for him to be there, and Lee woke several times with sweat on her forehead and her heart racing a hundred miles a minute, only calming down when she realised she was miles away in Devon.

* * *

The next day as she and Gina headed back to café to organise deliveries, Lee found herself constantly looking over her shoulder, wondering if Nathan would reappear. Did she want him to? She didn't think so, although she'd be lying if she hadn't considered what she would say if he actually did apologise properly, actually did beg for her to forgive him. The problem was, no matter how much she mulled it over in her mind, she wasn't sure what she would do if that actually did happen.

Then again, she didn't think it was likely to happen.

This was their final day of preparations before the big opening on Monday, and Lee found herself feeling proud of what they had achieved. Although the charm of the little café that she had fallen in love with remained, it looked fresh and vibrant - and definitely had a new stamp on it. Today was the day that Gina's sign was being fitted, and once again she felt lucky she'd met Gina, for she knew two people who could fit it that afternoon - and all for the promise of a free coffee on Monday.

Holding her breath, Lee watched as the two men finished fitting the sign, making sure it was straight and clear. She felt a bubble of excitement ripple through her as they finished and she read the sign: *Carol's Café.*

"Who's Carol then?" one of them - Mason, she thought he was called - asked, looking a little confused.

"She was my gran," Lee replied; "I always used to go to coffee shops with her, so it seemed fitting. Besides, I love a bit of alliteration!"

"Sounds good," he replied, dusting off his hands with a rag and packing away his tools.

"Oh, Lee, it looks wonderful." Lee whirled round to see Val stood, looking up at the café that had been hers for so many years.

"You think so?" Lee asked with a cautious smile. "I felt bad changing things…"

"Oh, shush, it needed updating and I couldn't face painting it, not with my old bones. No, it looks fantastic - I can't wait to come in on Monday for a cup of tea!"

Lee beamed - it was just what she'd needed to hear.

*   *   *

Opening day arrived drizzly and grey - but, since it was the first of December, Lee wasn't too surprised. She and Gina were at the café bright and early, making sure everything was ready. Both wore brand new aprons, with colourful cupcake patterns all over them. The coffee machine was on and ready to go, and Gina had spent several hours teaching Lee the basics of making a good coffee. While hers didn't look as artistic as Gina's - and she planned to take the orders and money and leave the actual barista work to Gina - she'd be able to make them at a push.

"Ready?" Gina asked as the clock struck eight, and Lee nodded. A blackboard was propped up on the counter with their opening offer - any drink and a cake for £5. With a nervous smile at one another, they turned the sign from 'closed' to 'open' and unlocked the door, ready for their first customers.

It was slow, at first; it was earlier than most of their friends would be up and about and in a coffee shop. But the rain worked in their favour, and slowly the trickle of customers (most of whom commented on the new decor and asked how long they'd been open) turned to a stream and by lunch time it was threatening to become a flood.

"Wow, Lee - it's packed!" Val's thin voice somehow rang out over all the chatter in the café; it was just after lunch time and nearly every table was full.

"Oh, Val, here, have this table," Lee said, quickly wiping down the only free table and directing Val to it. She glanced around at the tables full of every type of tea, coffee and hot chocolate, and grinned. "It's gone well! Lots of advertising for today though - I'm not expecting this every day. Still, it's nice to get our names out there!"

"It'll be all anyone can talk about - trust me," Val said, patting Lee on the hand. "Now, let me take a look at this menu, you get on with whatever you need to do."

The bell on the door rang as it opened again, and Lee nodded. "I'll be back in a minute!"

Back behind the counter, she turned to face the customer who had just walked in. He wore a police uniform, but carried the hat in his hand which let her see his curly, dark blond hair. She met his blue eyes and smiled, and was rewarded with a grin that showed off a gorgeous set of straight, white teeth.

"Hello, officer," she said, surprised to hear a hint of flirtation in her voice. "I hope there's nothing wrong?"

The tall man laughed a little, and then glanced up at the menu. "No, not unless you know something I don't! I was told I could get the best coffee around, so I thought I'd come in on my break and grab one. You only opened today, right?"

“That’s right,” Lee said with a grin. “And they are the best coffees.”

“What would you recommend?”

“How about a gingerbread macchiato? Especially for Christmas - unless you’re not feeling festive yet.”

“How could I not be feeling festive - the town lights are on, the tree is lit - I’ll take one.”

Gina began to make the drink without needing to be told; she and Lee had got into a rhythm today when they had been rushed off their feet and they were pleased to have made few mistakes.

The police officer counted out change to pay for the drink, and as Lee was ringing it into the till he spoke again; “You know, if you’re feeling festive, the Christmas market opens this evening. It always pretty magical…”

She didn’t feel the need to mention she already knew, or that she was already going; she simply smiled, and handed him his change. “Thanks.”

As he left with his coffee, Gina elbowed her sharply in the ribs. “What was that?” she asked with a grin.

“Nothing…” Lee said, blushing furiously. And it was nothing - her marriage had just fallen apart, there was no way she was looking for another man right now. Besides, she was getting ahead of herself - all she had done was a bit of casual flirting with a good looking police officer…

CHAPTER TEN

At five thirty, they locked the front door, turned the signs to closed and sat themselves down on the white, wooden chairs that they had freshly painted that week.

"I'm exhausted!" Gina exclaimed, but she was smiling all the same. Lee glanced at Gina and smiled; her hair was falling out of its messy bun, she had splatters of milk and coffee down her apron what looked like cake crumbs on her top. Had Lee seen herself in the mirror, she would have seen that she didn't look much different - messy, exhausted but elated.

"I can't believe how many people came!" Lee said, desperate for a cup of coffee but lacking the motivation to move and make one.

"I know a lot of people in this town and, besides, everyone loves somewhere new. Now we've just got to keep the business up. Have you counted how much we took?"

"Not yet," Lee admitted. She knew she wouldn't make a profit in the beginning - after all, she was the one paying the wages and paying for the redecorating - but she hoped that it wouldn't be long before it turned a small profit.

"I could fall asleep here," Gina admitted.

"We promised we'd go to the opening of the Christmas market!" Lee said, trying to get some energy back into her voice.

"I know, I know. You only want to go because PC Gorgeous might be there!" Lee batted her away and rolled her eyes.

"Please," she said, "I've got so much on my mind right now. It's just that we promised your friends, and I do love a Christmas market! Let's go home - I've got the car round the corner - and get showered, then go for half an hour or so. Then an early night before we're back in here tomorrow!" They'd planned to both work every day the first couple of weeks - then they would take it in turns so they could have time off. They were both too excited about the project for now to mind giving up all their free time.

"Oh okay, okay - but I'm keeping my eye out for PC Gorgeous, you know, just in case."

Lee didn't respond to that, but instead busied herself with locking up and setting the alarm. In truth, her mind was a jumbled mess; Nathan's sudden appearance over the weekend had shattered her carefully composed veneer of calm, and someone flirting with her had made her feel all sorts of feelings of guilt and confusion. As they walked to the car, they passed a tiny little wedding dress shop and Lee couldn't help her eye from wandering to the display in the window, and her mind from wandering back to her own wedding dress: white, A-line, covered in a delicate lace with a long train. She'd felt like the most important woman in the world in that dress; felt like her life was charmed. She had the job, she had the man, she had the gorgeous home…

Had being the operative word.

By the time they'd reached the car, Gina was asking her if she was okay as she was so quiet; Lee told her she was just tired, but the truth was much more complex.

Was she making a huge mistake, walking away from her seemingly charmed life because of a set back?

* * *

A hot shower gave her mind time to calm and her muscles time to ease from their day of hard graft. She couldn't remember the last time she had done such a physical day's work - and she hoped her body would cope with the shock of a job so different from sitting at her desk or representing people in court.

"Bathroom's free," she shouted to Gina, who had opted for the second shower before their trip into town for some well-earned mulled wine at the Christmas market. Back in her bedroom with a towel wrapped around her hair to keep it from dripping down her back, she shivered slightly and rifled through her growing collection of new, second hand and vintage clothes. Considering she'd arrived here with only the clothes on her back nearly three weeks previously, she'd amassed a decent enough range of clothes. A pair of black jeans and a slightly sparkly silver top were the choices she went with: smart, warm and a little bit festive. On a whim she chose some candy cane earrings that she'd bought in the market the previous week, before drying her hair quickly in an attempt to warm herself up. She glanced at the clock - six thirty, and they were meeting friends at seven. A quick listen out of her bedroom door told her Gina was still in the shower, and she decided to give Beth a quick call.

Perhaps she could reassure her that her crazy decisions were rooted in some sort of sanity.

She answered after the third ring - a good sign for someone who often let it ring off before ringing back ten minutes later, having forgotten to put her phone on loud. "Hey, Beth, it's me."

"Lee! I've been meaning to ring all week. How's things?"

"Honestly? I haven't a clue. But they're definitely busy…" Lee filled her in on the purchase of the lease, opening Carol's Café and their successful first day.

"What happened to my always-planning big sister?" Beth asked with a laugh. "You're more like me every day. Are you happy?"

"I'm happier than I was, does that count?"

"Definitely."

"I wasn't sure… I passed a wedding dress shop today. It made me think… and Nathan came here over the weekend."

"He did?? Why wasn't that the first thing you told me!"

"Oh Beth," Lee said with a sigh, running a hand through her freshly dried hair. "He just appeared, I wasn't expecting it… and he didn't even seem that apologetic, truth be told. He said he was sorry, but…"

"But?"

"I just felt like he was going through the motions. Doing what was expected." It was the first time she had admitted it out loud. "I told him I want a divorce."

"Good. Lee, he doesn't deserve you - you are worth ten of him. You do whatever it is that makes you happy - screw everyone else."

"I'm going to a Christmas market tonight - does that count?"

"For you, yes! Not for me - but you know I'm very bah humbug about these things."

"A cute police officer flirted with me today," Lee blurted out, without really planning to.

"Really!" Lee could almost picture the grin on Beth's face.

"Oh, stop, it was just flirting. But it was nice that someone might want to flirt with me."

"Shirley Jones, you are gorgeous, and don't you forget it. You'll have men falling over themselves to date you, when you want them to - trust me."

"You always say just what I need, sis. And I've decided to go back to my maiden name - I don't really want to hear Jones."

"Point taken. Anyway, enjoy your evening - I'll speak to you soon?"

"Definitely. Oh, and don't tell mum about the café! Love you."

"Love you too sis - and you know I always keep your secrets."

As they both hung up, Lee grinned, realising she felt a lot better than she had done before the phone call had begun.

* * *

Bells jingled in the background and Christmas was truly in the air thanks to a combination of CDs playing from shops that had stayed open late for the special opening of the market, carollers singing and a band that was just setting up to begin its festive set. Gina and Lee walked with their arms linked - something Lee had never really done with her female friends but that Gina seemed keen on with everyone. Gina's group of friends were waiting by the beautifully lit Christmas tree, which was a key location for a group of school-age carol singers. With hugs, hellos and congratulations on their first successful day of running a café, the group set off to peruse the small set of stalls that made up the town's market. White fairy lights hung from most of the displays, and through the mist they gave a sort of halo effect to the town square. The longest queue by far was at the mulled wine and hot chocolate stand, and so they decided to have a look at some of the gifts on offer before making their way there, in the hopes that the queue would have gone down.

“I love Christmas!” Lydia sighed as she picked up a hand-felted Santa Claus and glanced at the price. Lee was about to agree, as was her natural reaction to anything about the festive period, but paused for a second. She was trying very hard to take stock of her feelings in the moment - to make sure what she said or felt really was true to herself. For too long she felt that her feelings and decisions had not truly been her own.

After a couple of seconds, she grinned. “Me too!” Laughing at a hand-made cushion cover that said ‘Bah, Humbug!’, she fished out her purse and handed over a ten pound note; it was the perfect Christmas present for her Scrooge of a sister.

A few purchases and half an hour later, the group felt they had exhausted the delights of the Christmas market and were in need of a hard-earned cup of mulled wine. Fortunately, the crowd around the stall seemed to have subsided a little, and Lee and Gina only queued for a couple of minutes to get drinks for all their friends.

“Are you in charge of every drink in this town?” a smooth, deep voice asked from beside Lee. Attempting to balance three mugs of mulled wine, Lee turned to find herself face to face with the police officer from earlier in the day - but this time in civilian clothing. That curly, blond hair looked even darker in the dim light of the evening, and he wore black jeans and a knitted black jumper with Christmas stars embroidered on it.

Lee wasn’t sure how long she was silent for, but a jab in the ribs from Gina (which almost made her spill all her mugs of mulled wine) reminded her that she could not just stare - she needed to talk.

“Not all of them,” she managed to say, not feeling anywhere near as confident as she had done that afternoon in the glow of her new little café. “Just the good ones!”

“Can I have one of those?” he asked the man behind the stall. “And I’ll get these.” He handed over a twenty pound note despite Lee’s protests. Gina - who Lee hadn’t even noticed disappear - reappeared by her side and took the other two mugs of wine; then she was gone, leaving Lee, the police man and two mugs of gorgeous-smelling liquid.

“You really didn’t need to buy drinks for all of us,” Lee said, blushing a little - whether through nerves, embarrassment or because she really did think he was very good looking, she didn’t know.

“You served me the best coffee I’ve had in years - only way I could pay you back,” he said with a smile that lit up his eyes.

“Well, thank you,” Lee said, deciding not to argue.

“James,” he said, reaching out his hand.

“Lee,” she replied, taking his hand and feeling a delicious tingle where their fingers met. She’d forgotten what flirtation felt like!

“Nice to meet you, Lee. Since we’ve run into each other twice in one day, I thought we should know each other’s names. The café looks great - have you been in the business long?”

“Today was the first day we opened, so no, just a couple of weeks,” Lee said taking a sip of her mulled wine and regretting it when it burned her tongue. Trying to ignore the stinging in her mouth, her mind grasped desperately for something she could ask him.

“Do you work in Totnes often?”

"All over the South Hams," he replied. "You know what it's like, cuts all the time, we cover larger and larger areas. But I'm based in Totnes, and I live just outside."

Lee tried to think of something intelligent to say, but it seemed all thoughts had left her; she was pleased when he filled the gap with another question. "What got you into the café business then?"

"Oh, that's a long story," she said, not sure he needed to hear about her husband cheating on her right at this moment. "But the short version is that I'm a lawyer, and I decided to make some changes in my life and, well, here I am! For now, anyway."

"Wow!" James said, looking slightly bemused. "Lawyer to café owner - quite a jump."

"Mmm," she said. "I'm enjoying it though - but we'll see what happens." She was sure to make it clear that she was not here for the long run; she wasn't sure why, but she didn't want anyone thinking that she would always be around. She knew this was just temporary; time for her to get over her life being torn to pieces before she went back and rebuilt it. A time out; a breather. Not the plan for the rest of her life. Although, at the moment, she didn't know what that plan looked like.

"It's great you decided to just follow what you wanted - so many people get stuck in something they hate. At the minute I love my job - I hope I'd be as brave as you if I ever stopped feeling like that."

Lee considered his words for a moment; was she brave? Or just stupid? She'd definitely been one of those people who pushed on with things even if she wasn't really that happy… but this decision hadn't been planned. It had just sort of… happened.

They talked until their mulled wine ran out and Lee mentioned that she should be getting back to her friends.

"It was lovely to see you again," James said, with a sincere smile and the lightest of touches of his hand to her upper arm. "Would you like to have dinner sometime?"

Lee took a sharp intake of breath. She hadn't been expecting it - in spite of their flirting, she hadn't thought he would actually ask her out. "I would love to," she said, "but I can't. I'm sorry."

"Okay," he said, looking a little disappointed but not letting it change his warm tone. "Can I ask why? Tell me to go away if I'm being pushy."

"Go away! No, no, I'm joking. My… my marriage just fell apart. It's the reason for the change… and I can't date right now."

James nodded for a moment, a hint of stubble clear on his chin under the light of the moon and the Christmas lights. "That's fair enough, although I won't say I'm not disappointed." Lee smiled; it was nice to know that someone wanted to take her for dinner, even though she knew she wasn't ready for a step like that. "But I hope to see you around - maybe we can have a drink again. As friends?"

"I'd like that," Lee said. Then, without planning her words, she blurted out: "I could give you my number?"

"Definitely." They swapped numbers before Lee could even think about what she was doing, and then James was holding his hand out again for her to shake it.

"Thanks for a lovely evening, Lee." They shook hands, which felt oddly formal, and Lee wondered if he felt that same frisson as the tips of their fingers met.

And then he was gone, into the darkness, and Lee's head felt full of a million different thoughts and feelings.

The week passed by in a blur of early mornings, frothy coffees and a lot of customers, and by Sunday Lee was exceptionally pleased they'd decided to close on Sundays for the foreseeable future. Her body ached in ways she didn't know was possible - but she had slept well every night since Monday night. Monday night had been a different story… she had spent it rehashing the conversations she'd had in the day with James, and questioning her decision that she couldn't go to dinner with him… maybe she could, maybe just as friends? Then her mind got all churned up again, and so sleep had evaded her for most of the night.

The rest of the week, however, she had been too exhausted for that. After a hot shower and some dinner, she'd been in bed early every night, falling into a deep and mostly dreamless sleep the moment her head hit the pillow. Whilst they hadn't been as heaving as that first day, there'd been steady trickle of customers all day with a lull at around four in the afternoon, for which they were already planning on how to drive in some more customers. Lee was confident that, when she got a moment to have a look at the books, they wouldn't disappoint her. She could afford to live for a little while without earning, and she was surprised to realise that the lack of certainty about her income didn't stress her. She knew she was okay for now; she knew she had a well-paying job to go back to. For the moment, she could focus on throwing her all into this business. Besides, she wasn't ready yet to think about going back - even though it had been three weeks since she'd first turned up in this eccentric little town.

It was halfway through the second week - when she'd told Gina to take a day off, and that she could run the café by herself for a day, that two people who knew Lee by name turned up.

One was James, the cute police officer.

One was her mother.

*   *   *

It was a Wednesday morning, and Lee was in by seven, baking homemade scones ready to serve cream teas in the afternoon. There was a delivery of the other cakes they had decided to stock that week from the local bakery, and Lee enjoyed having a chat with the teenager delivering them before he headed off to college. As she weighed out her ingredients, she pondered this routine she had managed to fall into - it was like she was living a different person's life, and yet it was beginning to feel like her own. The problem with being at work alone was that it gave her too much time to think; time to think about when she should head home, when she should file divorce papers, when she should confront Nathan about their finances, when she should ring her colleagues and update them on her life… the list was endless.

So wrapped up in her own thoughts was she, she didn't think to check her phone that morning. When she eventually did an hour later, she had three missed calls and a text that said. *'Sorry, mum knows about the café and is on her way - not my fault! Sorry! B xxx'*

But she didn't; and so the pounding knock on the door twenty minutes before she was due to open surprised her. Glancing in the mirror above the fireplace as she left the kitchen, she realised she had flour on her face and a few tendrils of hair falling out of the bun she had thrown it up into early this morning. She wiped the flour away, thinking that she could sort her hair later, and headed towards the door. It was only when she opened it that she realised it was her own mother; she was so surprised to see her in this setting that it hadn't even occurred to her that the petite blonde lady in the dim early morning light could possibly be her mother.

"Shirley!" her mother exclaimed, throwing her arms around her before Lee's brain had enough time to catch up with the events. "Well finding you has been a mission, hasn't it."

Lee stepped out of the way, letting her mother in, and locked the door behind her. She only had twenty minutes, but the last thing she wanted was a customer walking in a little early and finding her in a heated conversation with her mother.

"Hey mum," Lee said, taking a seat at a table, presuming she was in for a lecture. It wasn't that she didn't love her mother; her, Beth and her mum had always got on fairly well, both before and after her father had walked out. In fact, for the last few years, Lee had maintained a far easier relationship with their mother than Beth had. She'd made the choices that Tina wanted for her daughters: a steady career, a nice house, a supposedly happy marriage. Other than having a baby, she always appeared to approve of Lee's choices in a way she didn't of Beth's free spirit.

And that was why Lee knew she was in for a lecture; for so long her decisions had been the 'right' ones. Now that she had made her somewhat more questionable decisions, she didn't think her mother would approve. And one thing Tina Davis never did was hold her tongue.

"Hey mum indeed! Do you know how much I had to get on at your sister before she'd give me this address? You're my daughter for goodness sake, I haven't seen you in a month, everything in your life changes and you don't even tell me where you are? What is this place, anyway?"

"Oh mum," Lee said, feeling the tears begin to slide down her cheeks.

"Now, now, Shirley, don't cry," Tina said, stroking her arm slightly awkwardly. Since their father left, she had always struggled with open displays of emotion. Perhaps it was the weeks of crying that had followed his sudden departure that had put her off…

"I've bought the lease. I'm running this place…"

"You're running it? When your sister gave me this address I thought you lived here, maybe were working a few shifts… is this… a permanent move then?"

"No. Well… I don't think so, anyway. No, I've got a job back home, I've told them I'm going back. Things just got so messed up, mum. Nathan…"

"I know. And I've given Nathan more than one piece of my mind, believe me. There is always the option to work on it, see a counsellor, see if you can fix things… but no, I can see that's not an option." Lee didn't know if her mother had come to that conclusion before she'd arrived, or whether the glare from Lee had made her hastily change her words, but she was right; there was no going back now. Not to her marriage, anyway.

"Things have fallen apart, mum, and I just need to get my head straight."

"Three weeks down here though, Shirley, surely it's time to come back to real life now? You can't stay hidden down here for much longer. Come home for Christmas, at least."

"I'll think about it, mum. Anyway," she stood, hoping to hint to her mum that she needed to get on, but her mum did not move. "I've got to open up, mum."

"We need to talk, Shirley. I'm worried about you." Never one to mince her words, Tina stood and looked her tall daughter straight in the eye.

"I finish at half five."

"I'll see you then."

The goodbye was stilted, but Lee did lean down and kiss her mum on the cheek as she left. Then she turned round the open sign, rubbed the tears from her eyes and took a deep breath to try to get her day back on track.

* * *

It was another busy day, and Lee tried to put her mother and the discussion they were bound to have at the end of the day to the back of her mind. The rhythms of the café made it surprisingly easy to forget: there was a steady stream of customers, most of whom wanted to have a chat about their day, what was going on in Totnes and their plans for the festive period. The repeated actions of heating the milk, grinding the coffee and taking the money kept her mind occupied for most of the day. She wasn't looking forward to the standard four o'clock lull; they had plans for kids' happy hour hot chocolates over the holidays, but they wouldn't start for a couple of weeks and today of all days she didn't need half an hour for her thoughts to take over. Whenever she did have a pause, she felt on the brink of tears; she blamed her mother's appearance for her turbulent emotional state.

She lost track of time over the afternoon rush, where many people who were fast becoming regulars came in for fresh, homemade scones, jam and cream. There was often a debate over which order they were put on - Lee had learned that putting the cream first was the Devon way, whereas the jam first was the Cornish way - and people felt surprisingly strongly about the topic! And so the four o'clock lull snuck up on her and before she knew it the café was unexpectedly empty and still. She took a deep breath and surveyed it; a few tables to wipe, some sweeping to do before a few people would probably stop in for a cup of tea or coffee after they'd been at work. She was finding they were perfectly placed between the shops and the odd office or two, and the nearest long stay car park; they easily seemed to tempt a few in for a quick cuppa before heading home.

She was busy diligently sweeping the crumbs from the corners of the room when the bell tinkled to signal the door opened. Lee turned with her waitress-smile on (which was very similar to her client smile, or even her in-laws smile) which instantly became genuine when she saw who was at the door.

James stood in his smart black uniform, head not far off the door frame, blond curls slightly mussed from where she presumed his hat had sat before he entered.

"Hi," she said, unsure why more words weren't forthcoming.

"Hi," he said, with a wide smile. "Am I okay to come in for a coffee?"

"Of course," Lee said, brushing a few crumbs off her hands onto her apron and walking back behind the counter. "We are a café after all!"

"No, I meant… I didn't want to make you feel awkward, asking you for dinner and then turning up here after you'd said no. It's not that I won't take no for an answer, I promise. I just… really wanted another of your coffees."

Lee smiled, and couldn't help but hope coffee wasn't his only motivation for coming into the café. "Thanks for being so considerate but you're welcome any time."

"Good." He pulled a stool up to the counter so he was sat opposite Lee, and took a seat. "Will you have one with me? I'm buying!"

"Don't be silly," Lee said. "We'll have them on the house."

It seemed natural to pull a chair behind the counter, so that they were both sat enjoying their coffees together. As they chatted about how quiet town always was at this time of day, Lee remembered that her hair had been falling all over the place first thing that morning - she dreaded to think what it looked like now. She tried to slowly slide her chair so that she could see herself in the mirror above the now-decorative fireplace opposite, but when she nearly toppled over and had to grab the counter for support, she aborted the plan and hoped that she didn't look too repulsive. Then she chastised herself for even caring; she'd told this poor, gorgeous, funny man that she couldn't date him - and she knew that was true - so it didn't matter what she looked like. In fact, the more repulsive the better.

Well, maybe that was taking it a step too far.

"Is there much crime in Totnes today then?" Lee asked, sipping on her sweet coffee topped with cinnamon.

"Oh, plenty. Pulled someone over this morning for having a broken brake light… knocked on some doors in relation to some missing property…"

"Oh, high crime then!"

"Indeed. But I'm glad - gave me time to stop off here."

Lee blushed and looked down at her coffee, lost for words yet again.

"I'm sorry," James said, running a hand through his hair a little nervously. "That was too flirtatious. It just slipped out."

Lee glanced up at his face, chin covered in a hint of light stubble, broad lips that looked like they were just made for- "It's okay. Honestly," she said, in a hurry to stop the direction of her thoughts.

"Can I ask you a question? Even though this is only the third time we've met?"

“I guess…” Lee said, a little apprehensive. “Although, be warned, I might have a flood of customers in a minute and then I’ll be far too busy for you.”

“Okay, consider me warned. Can I ask - what happened with your marriage? It’s just… oh, I don’t know. I feel like talking to you is so easy, and you seem so sure of what you want in life, and go and grab it when you do - I’m quite envious of that. I’m not sure whether I’m a police officer because I wanted to be, or because I dressed up as a police officer when I was five and it was all my mum ever went on about after that point. I guess what I’m saying is, you impress me, and intrigue me, and I’ve wondered since the other night what caused you to be so definite that you couldn’t date.” He took a pause for breath, and Lee sat quite speechless at his words. “Sorry,” he added. “I babble on a bit when I’m nervous.”

For a moment she considered fobbing him off with some excuse; she felt almost embarrassed to admit that Nathan had cheated on her, as though it reflected badly on her. She felt in some way that it showed she was lacking; that there was something in her that was so awful, Nathan had needed to go elsewhere.

But James had been so open and honest with her about his reasons, and he was right; talking did feel easy with him, when the words found their way from her mouth! And so she took a deep breath, and said the words she had so rarely said out loud:

“He cheated on me. I got home and found him… in bed with another woman.”

“Shit. I’m sorry - that sucks.”

“And I got in a car and… drove here.”

“Seriously?”

Lee gave a wan smile and nodded. "Seriously. Walked in on them together last month, found out she wasn't the first and got in the car. I haven't been back since - and somehow I now have a flat and the lease on a café. Believe me, I'm not usually the spontaneous, go and get whatever it is you want type. I'm the sort of girl who has a five year plan, hell a ten year plan, and sticks to it religiously. I'm the woman who thought she had the husband sorted, the house sorted, would tick kids off the list soon - well, I was that sort of woman." She shrugged, realising all of a sudden that she had shared far more than was appropriate and that tears were welling up in her eyes. She blinked furiously, hoping James hadn't spotted them. "And now I'm the crazy woman babbling on far too much about her ex to someone she barely knows!"

James shook his head. "Not crazy. I think you're incredibly brave." For a moment their eyes met, and Lee couldn't remember the last time anyone else had called her something as wonderful as 'brave'. It sounded a whole lot better than 'stupid'. She felt something crackle between them as their eyes were locked for longer than was strictly comfortable; the tension was almost visible in the air.

James lifted his hand towards her, and as she wondered what he was doing, he murmured: "You've got flour on your cheek. Do you mind?" Lee didn't have the breath to speak, and as his fingers lightly brushed against her cheek she had to tell herself sternly not to close her eyes and melt into him. Without knowing who initiated it, both their heads moved forwards across the counter, almost of their own accord, moved by the magic that was in the air at that moment.

And then the front door opened and two businessmen in smart black suits walked in. James and Lee jumped apart, and, without glancing back at him, Lee hopped up off the stool to serve the men.

Neither said anything about what had passed between them, and as Lee busied herself with the now-familiar tasks of steaming milk and preparing the coffee, James downed the dregs of his drink.

"See you around?" he said softly, his inflection questioning whether this was the end of any sort of friendship with them. It was then that Lee turned and their eyes met for just a second; she nodded with a blush, and was rewarded with a grin from him as he left the building.

Lee was sure her heart didn't stop hammering until she locked up the shop at closing time.

CHAPTER ELEVEN

The afternoon chat with James had almost made her forget that her mother was in town, doing goodness knows what as she waited for Lee to finish work. She hadn't reappeared during the day, which Lee had been surprised by but - sure enough - as she exited the building having turned all the lights off and locked up, her mother was stood waiting under an umbrella on the opposite side of the street.

Umbrella-less, Lee pulled the hood of her coat over her head to protect against the drizzle, and dashed across the road at the first available opportunity between the stream of cars heading home for the night.

"Where have you been all day?" she asked her mum, ducking under the umbrella and linking arms with her mum - a definite learned behaviour from Gina.

"Oh you know - a bit of shopping, wandered through the market, had lunch, then booked into that hotel across the road - I don't feel like a three hour drive tonight. And since I don't even know where you're staying down here…"

"The hotel's probably best mum, I live in a shared flat with no spare bedroom."

Tina stopped abruptly and turned to face her daughter, annoying the pedestrians behind her who were forced to alter their route to continue up Fore Street. "What has happened to you, Shirley? Shared flats and cafés?"

"My husband cheated on me," Lee said simply, for the second time that day. "Come on mum, we're getting soaked, let's get an early dinner and we can talk then." They continued up the hill, just as a man in open shoes and what Lee thought were pyjama bottoms pushed his way past them. She grinned slightly as she saw her mum look him up and down, but there was no comment.

The little restaurant half way up the town was not busy due to the early hour, and Lee and her mum were seated quickly in a cosy table lit with three candles. Feeling like she would probably need it, Lee ordered a large glass of wine despite her mum declining, and they ordered some bread and olives to start.

"Your sister's worried about you," Tina threw into the conversation as the wine arrived.

"She is not!" Lee scoffed. "This is exactly the sort of thing she would do, and you know it."

"Well, she did say it's very unlike you."

"Which it is. But I needed a change, and this is it. I don't know why people can't just accept that…"

"But you are going back to Bristol? And the law firm?"

"Yes, mother." She sighed and rolled her eyes, something she didn't think she'd done since being a teenager. "I spoke to Tania yesterday. They're holding down the fort quite happily without me and have suggested I extend my… sabbatical until after Christmas. Start fresh in the new year."

That wasn't entirely true; while they were coping fine without Lee, they had assumed she would be back before Christmas. It had been Lee who had put them off; Lee who couldn't imagine Christmas day anywhere but Totnes; Lee who thought that she would cope better if she had a clean slate in a new year.

"I'll start looking for somewhere to live this week," she said, feeling slightly sick at the thought.

“How are you affording all this?” her mother asked bluntly as their appetisers arrived.

“I’ve got savings.”

“For a rainy day, Lee, not for buying a café on a whim.”

“I’m only leasing it,” Lee answered, glancing outside and laughing at the irony as rain battered the windows and poured off the guttering. “Besides, I’d say my marriage breaking up is a pretty rainy day. And I will get over it - I just needed some time.” She paused, and the bravado in her voice dropped. “It was a big shock,” she said quietly.

“I know,” Tina said. “I know.” She tapped Lee on the hand, before rattling out her order to the waiting waitress. Lee added hers and hoped that the lecture was over.

“Just promise me, please, that you won’t waste your life down here? You have so much Lee, and I know this has been a setback, but you will recover. You will meet someone else, you will have children…”

The word made tears prick Lee’s eyes for the countless time that day; that was the real sore point, she thought. The fact that there’d been a plan; the fact that she wasn’t getting any younger and now she would have to start all over again with meeting someone, falling in love, marrying, getting them to agree the time was right to have children…

Maybe, she thought, not every man needed persuading. Maybe she could meet someone who was as keen as she was to have kids. Who she also loved. And who understood the number of hours she worked, and wouldn’t use that as an excuse to start sleeping around…

She felt her shoulders slump - it felt like more and more of a tall order as she allowed the requisites to swirl around in her mind.

* * *

She left her mum in the hotel quite late by her current standards, and began to hike up the hill to her flat as she'd made the decision to walk to work that morning. The Christmas lights glowed bright against their dark and misty background, and Lee found they lifted her spirits a little. She wasn't sure if seeing her mum had been a good thing or a bad thing; on the one hand, she loved her mum, and she had given her at least a little sympathy. But it had sent her brain down a dangerous path that she'd been trying to block: the path of what if.

What if she gave Nathan another chance? If he swore blind it would never happen again, perhaps she could get past it eventually. She could move back to their home, the house she'd loved so much, put her heart and soul into decorating. They wouldn't have to go through the messy business (and as a lawyer, she should know) of a divorce; they could discuss kids again, open up the lines of communication, bring back the romance.

She could. It was possible. Yes, the people she'd told about the affair would think she was crazy - but she was fairly sure they thought she was having a breakdown right this minute, so that wouldn't be so different. It would certainly be easier than starting life all over again when she would be turning 31 the next month and had thought everything was lined up perfectly in front of her.

As she started to run out of breath from the steepness of the hill and the pace at which she was pushing herself to get up it, her thoughts turned to romance. She tried to imagine kissing Nathan, removing his clothes, being naked in front of him - but, try as she might, the images didn't work in her head. Time and time again she saw the blonde in her place, and when she did succeed in picturing Nathan trying to kiss her, she felt a kind of repulsion that shocked her with its force.

When she put her key into the lock, her brain hadn't yet sorted out her emotions from the dinner with her mother. It had certainly stirred up all sorts of thoughts and feelings that she'd been fairly successfully repressing. She found herself relieved that Gina either wasn't up or wasn't home; she wasn't in the mood to chat about work, or their now kind of shared friendship group. Exhausted, she put off showering until the next day and slid beneath the cool duvet, shivering slightly despite enjoying the chill of the bedding on her sore and aching muscles - not to mention her confused mind.

*　　*　　*

It was the first fitful night's sleep she'd had in a couple of weeks, and she found herself awake at 6am, a full hour before her alarm was set to go off. For a while she lay and stared at the ceiling, trying to decide whether to get her shower over and done with or to attempt to get a little more shut-eye. Before she had made her mind up, she decided to check her phone, and the message there sent more sleep straight off the table.

When are you back in Bristol? The text read. It was from Nathan, though he hadn't signed it. There were also, she noticed immediately, no kisses.

After Christmas.

She didn't wait long for his reply; she had lost track of his schedule weeks earlier, and so she wasn't sure if he was just getting up or just getting to bed.

You're staying down there for Christmas?

Her mind was made up in an instant; she couldn't picture Christmas elsewhere. She did not want to be surrounded by family and reminders of what her life would have been - that might just drain the Christmas magic, even from Lee. No, here she didn't really have a past; here she could enjoy the festive spirit, even if it would probably be alone - although she hadn't discussed Gina's Christmas plans with her yet.

Yes. Short, simple and to the point - she didn't see the need to give him any more than that.

Didn't want to say this by text but you're not taking my calls. Wanted you to know I'm seeing someone. Will you take care of the divorce? Such simple words, sat there in black and white on her phone screen in front of her - words that, nonetheless, felt like a dagger to her heart. She took a sharp intake of breath as she read them and couldn't quite believe how harsh they looked in print. No, she hadn't taken his calls, because she had nothing to say - but to see their marriage ended in the blocky letters of a text message she thought might have broken her heart.

No, her heart had already been broken by his infidelity; this was just rubbing salt in the wound.

I'm seeing someone.

The blonde? The nurse? A doctor? Or someone completely new? Had they overlapped with their marriage? Had they consummated whatever relationship they had in her marital bed?

Questions she didn't even want to know the answers to buzzed round her head like flies, and the room in front of her began to look a little hazy.

Knowing she needed to calm down a little, she closed her eyes and took several deep breaths, attempting to send those words from her brain.

So this was it. No more options, no more choices; he was done. And as much as she knew that she had been done the moment she saw him and that woman, she still cried her way through the hottest shower she could handle.

* * *

"Can you open up on your own today?" Lee asked Gina when they met over the toaster an hour later.

"Sure - everything okay? You were late last night."

"My mum turned up… and Nathan text. My head's just all over the place - I just need an hour or so to get my head together."

Gina didn't push the topic; instead she poured boiling water into both their mugs and said, "If you want to talk, I'm here."

"I appreciate that," Lee said, tears prickling in her eyes that she desperately tried to blink away. She waited until Gina had left for them to fall, and tried to accept that she needed to mourn the end of everything she'd thought her life would be for a little while. It was the permanent shutting and locking of a door that she realised she'd always thought was still ajar - if she wanted it to be. Dressed and ready for work, she let herself wallow for a little while, curling up on the sofa and not fighting the tears.

She gave herself nearly an hour to cry, and inwardly rant, and to write (and then delete) several expletive laden texts to Nathan before heading down to the café, all the while trying to convince herself that this wasn't anything new; she had known it was over. This couldn't break her heart all over again, because it had already been broken.

Part of her wanted to see her mum and sob in her arms; part of her knew it was better that she had left early that morning. She didn't want to hear reasons why she should consider going back to Nathan again - especially now that he obviously wouldn't be interested any more. She thought her mum had got the message - but she wouldn't put it past her to think of another couple of reasons why her marriage was something worth saving.

What a mess it all was.

CHAPTER TWELVE

A week flew by without Lee really knowing where it had gone; over halfway through December and Lee felt like the Christmas spirit that had always been a part of this month for her had flown the nest. She served coffees, teas and cakes; she discussed the big news in town that there was a possibility of snow the following week; she told Gina she was fine - but inside she felt like she'd gone as cold as the wintry weather.

"Is everything okay dear?" Val asked one day when she came in for a coffee and a scone. It was a quiet afternoon and Lee had found herself staring out at a family walking past the window, smiling and laughing in their big coats and scarves.

"Sorry? Oh yes, I'm fine."

"You don't seem to have the same sparkle as you did at the beginning of the month. I hope this place isn't exhausting you already."

Lee gave a slightly sad smile. "Oh, no. This place gives me a reason to get up in the mornings." As she said the words, she was struck with how true they really were.

"A young, energetic, gorgeous girl like you? You need more in your life than just this place - no matter how much the locals rave about it."

"You flatter me! I'm not that young, and definitely not that energetic. And I'm not sure you'd find that many people who would agree with the last part, either."

The bell on the door tinkled as a cold blast of air entered the café. Stood in the door way in dark jeans, a black knitted jumper and a tartan scarf, was James.

Lee didn't have time to think about the fact that she felt warm inside for the first time in days before Val began to speak.

"James! How lovely to see you dear, and on your day off. Come and pull a seat up next to me and agree with me."

James laughed, a deep throaty chuckle that filled the café and made Lee smile against her will. "Of course, Mrs Thomas. May I ask what I'm agreeing with you on?"

"That Lee here - have you met her? You should, she's fantastic. Anyway, my statement was that Lee is gorgeous, and she disagreed with me - which, as you well know, I don't tend to accept. So you have to agree with me."

"Oh, I do," he said; Lee felt her cheeks burn red and almost wished the ground would swallow her up. She loved Val, truly - but asking the guy that she undeniably had a crush on whether he found her gorgeous was still extremely embarrassing. "She is most definitely, completely, utterly gorgeous."

"There," Val said, with a grin, seeming oblivious to Lee's discomfort. "It's settled."

"Can I get you a drink?" Lee asked, feeling as though she couldn't make eye contact with him; instead her eyes hovered slightly lower, although the danger in that was that she could see a hint of his defined muscles through his thin jumper and they didn't help the direction her thoughts were heading…

"A Christmas coffee, please - surprise me with one."

"Coming right up," Lee said, pleased for an excuse to turn around and give the fire in her cheeks a chance to die down.

"I'd better get home, it's dark so early and I like to be in with the fire lit before it's pitch black!" Val said. "What do I owe you Lee?"

"You know your money's no good here," Lee said as she served a candy cane macchiato for James. As usual, Val tutted and put down a fiver on the counter, refusing to take no for an answer. "And you, PC Knight, should pop round and see me sometime. I used to see you all the time when you were growing up next door, and now you move two minutes out of town and I only see you when you're on duty!"

Lee watched out of the corner of her eye as he gave her a bright smile that lit up his whole face, and in turn hers. "Of course I will Mrs Thomas. Take care."

She busied herself with wiping down the sides and beginning to turn off the coffee machine; she had only just realised that it was nearing closing time. She'd suggested Gina head home early as they were quiet enough at this time of day for Lee to comfortably manage on her own, and Gina had been keen to go and get some Christmas shopping done. When she turned to glance at the clock, she realised it was just James and her in the little café. The sky outside had quickly turned from midnight blue to black, and the Christmas lights outside twinkled prettily through the condensation on the windows.

"Nice?" she asked him, as he sipped the sweet Christmassy drink she'd prepared for him.

"Delicious," he said. "Very sweet - it's filling me with the joy of Christmas!"

"Maybe I'll have to make myself one then - I seem to have lost that lately." The words were so honest, and they slipped out before she'd even realised she was saying them. That seemed to happen quite regularly around James.

“Why’s that?” he asked, and she found the way he was looking at her made her feel as though he could see right through the cheerful facade she had been putting on for the customers, for Gina, even for herself. “I thought you loved this time of year.”

“I do… I did. My life just isn’t as simple as it was - it makes it hard to find the magic like I used to.”

“It’s always there, I think - just sometimes it takes a little bit more searching to find it.”

“Maybe,” Lee said, not sure she could agree. Maybe some things just stripped the magic away. “I’m sorry but I’ve got to start locking up.”

“Sorry, I didn’t realise - can I help?”

“You’re a customer!” Lee said with a laugh. “You don’t need to help.”

“I don’t mind,” he said, reaching over and grabbing the cloth. “I enjoy the company.”

“If you say so,” Lee said, rolling her eyes a little and packing away the cakes in their airtight containers as James began wiping down the tables. She carried them into the small back room and took a deep breath; she was a thirty year old woman (with thirty one fast approaching!), she did not need to be mindless and giggly around a boy she liked. Man she liked. Man she kept picturing with his lips on hers…

Shaking her head to try to remove that undoubtedly pleasant image, Lee reached up to the fourth shelf in the wooden slatted shelving rack to put the cakes away and suddenly found a bag of flour toppling straight for her. In her distracted state she had knocked the baking ingredients to the far edge of the shelf and, unfortunately, the messiest had been the one to fall. It was too late to do anything - she tried to block the flour with her hands but in seconds she and the floor were absolutely covered.

"Great," she muttered, shaking her head so the worst of the white powder fell from her hair and face. "Just marvellous."

"Is everything all right?" a resonating voice called from the café, and she realised she'd forgotten for a second that James was in the building. '*Brilliant,*' she thought. '*Just what he needs to see - me covered in flour.*'

She tried to insist that everything was fine, but moments later he appeared in the doorway, took one look at her and burst into laughter.

"What happened?" he said when he had collected himself. "It looks like it's been snowing here!"

"Oh, it's not that funny!" Lee said, feeling slightly irritated by the whole event. "I knocked the flour off the shelf when I put the cakes on. So stupid, I wasn't paying enough attention." She ran her fingers through her hair, trying to get the flour that was clinging on to the blonde strands to fall to the ground, then realised her shoulders were covered and did a little shimmy before realising she must look ridiculous.

"Here, let me," James said, and she didn't have time to protest before his large hands were on her head, dusting the flour from her. She felt a warmth shoot through her that shocked her with its intensity; she was frozen to the spot, unable to speak, unable to think about anything but the fact that the top of his broad chest was right in her eye line and his hands were on her head, on her shoulders. She moved her eyes just a fraction to look up at him and as their eyes met it was as though the whole world stopped around her. Nothing mattered in that moment - just her, him and the pounding of her heart that she was sure was loud enough for him to hear.

One hand dropped from her shoulder to her waist without a word being spoken; the other was in her hair, palm to her cheek. Despite Lee's height there was a decent amount of difference between their heads, and without knowing who moved first they were both moving towards one another. Lee stopped thinking about anything but his lips as they slowly, gently, sweetly pressed against hers. A jolt of something that felt like lightening shot from where their lips met to every part of her body, and what followed was not slow, nor sweet, nor gentle. Forgetting the flour completely, Lee reached up and threw her arms around his neck, pulling him closer to her. His hand on her waist became a little rougher, pulling her tightly towards him until there wasn't a centimetre between their bodies. His hand remained in her hair, tipping her head upwards toward him and their lips met once more, passionately moving as though their very lives depended on it. A step backwards and Lee was being pressed into the shelving unit; she could feel the hard slats of wood behind her and his warm, soft yet toned body in front of her. She focused on feeling, feeling every one of these exhilarating sensations as their tongues met and she suppressed a groan of desire.

Neither heard the tinkle of the doorbell as it swung open, nor the footsteps in the café. They heard nothing until -

"Lee? Are you here? I realised I left my phone, I was going to ring you and ask you to bring it home but then, dur I realised I didn't have a-"

She stopped dead in the doorway of the store cupboard, where Lee and James had not had time to extricate themselves from the embrace. Both were red and flushed and totally out of breath, and for a moment no-one said anything.

"Shit," Gina said. "Sorry, I didn't mean to interrupt, I'll just-" It was testament to the surprising nature of the situation that she didn't even comment on the fact that they were both covered in flour. She turned on her heel, grabbed her phone and left, leaving James and Lee in close proximity with an awkward silence surrounding them.

"Well…" James said, taking a step back and running a hand through his now floury hair. "That wasn't expected."

Lee shook her head. "No…" She tried to smile, afraid that he would think that she wasn't happy with the situation - because, despite what she'd said being true, she didn't think she'd ever been so turned on in her life.

"I'm sorry, I know you said-"

"Don't be," Lee interrupted, putting her hand out to grab his; his eyes shot up to meet hers. "I mean… god I'm confused. I can't get involved in anything right now, it's all too mixed up. But that kiss… please never apologise for that."

James grinned, and Lee almost wished he would kiss her that thoroughly all over again. "Okay. No apology. No pressure."

"This may be a huge mistake but… would you like to go for a drink tomorrow night? To chat?"

"Sounds great." He leant forward and pressed his lips to hers; a chaste, soft kiss this time, nothing like the fire that burned through them moments before - although Lee had a suspicion that that fire could be rekindled in seconds if any kind of contact between them continued. The attraction sparked around them like electricity.

"You'd better go or I'll never get cleared up," Lee said with a rueful smile.

"I could help…"

"Look where that got us!" Strangely, it seemed that her tongue had loosened around him, now that - well, now that it had so thoroughly explored his mouth!

"Fair enough," he said with a shrug. "Until tomorrow, then."

Once she'd heard the front door close, she leant back against the unit and closed her eyes, taking a few deep, calming breaths to still her furiously beating heart. She hadn't a clue what she was doing, but god it had felt good.

Clearing up took longer than she had planned, thanks to the flour, and she spent the time thinking about what on earth she was going to say to Gina - who, she knew, would want a full explanation of the compromising position she had been found in.

CHAPTER THIRTEEN

Lee had the chilly walk home to try and figure out what she wanted, what this all meant - and what she was going to tell Gina. If she hadn't walked in on them, what would have happened? Could she enter a relationship with someone? What about just a fling? But then was that fair to James?

She couldn't help but go round and round these questions, finding another unanswerable question every time she tried to reach a conclusion. The one plus side, she realised, was it stopped that sinking sadness she'd been feeling this week; reliving that kiss in her mind was definitely enough to banish the cold and miserable feelings.

As soon as her key was in the door, Gina was out of her chair.

"I want answers!" she said, flicking the kettle switch on and getting out two mugs. "Sit down and don't even think about saying you're tired, that was the hottest kiss I think I've ever seen."

Lee laughed in spite of herself, and sunk into the cosy arm chair, waiting for Gina to bring over the cup of tea she was making.

"Oh Gina," she said. "I don't know what to do!"

"About what?"

"This! Him!"

"Is the answer of 'bang his brains out' too obvious? Because I'm struggling to see the issue here."

"Gina! You can't say that!" Lee said with a little giggle.

"I definitely can. So, how long has this been going on?"

"Nothing really is going on," Lee said, sipping her tea. "We've flirted a bit, I guess and then… he offered to help clear up, I dropped flour everywhere, he tried to get it out of my hair-"

"And you ended up pressed against the store room shelves!"

"Pretty much! God, Gina, the chemistry is electric. I'm just drawn to him like I've never been drawn to anyone before. He walks in and I can't think straight, he looks at me and I blush, he kisses me and…"

"You want to bang his brains out," Gina finished with a smirk.

"Well, I wouldn't put it like that, but yes, that's pretty much the gist of it."

"So what's the problem?"

"My marriage has just fallen apart. I spent last week crying on the sofa because he'd told me he was dating someone else. I don't think I'm emotionally ready to date anyone - and certainly not anything serious."

"Ok," Gina said, clearly mulling this over in her mind as she drank her tea. "Well, tell him that. Tell him you think he's amazingly sexy, and you want to-"

"We don't need to say it again!" Lee interrupted.

"Okay, okay, but that you're not ready for something committed and so it can only be casual. See what he says - he might be fine with that. With chemistry like that flying between you, I bet he'll accept it. And then you can see how it goes."

"I guess," Lee said, shrugging. "It terrifies me a bit. I've not dated in years. Not slept with anyone other than - than Nathan in such a long time. I feel so out of practice with that whole world."

"Lee, that's the fun bit. The awkwardness, the hours of kissing, the passionate sex… believe me, you'll be fine once you take the plunge. I couldn't believe when I walked in and there you two were, tangled up in one another and covered in flour… I hate to think what I would have walked in on if I'd been ten minutes later!"

Lee didn't answer, but she silently agreed with Gina's assessment; she had no control of her thoughts around James. Having sex in the store cupboard of the café certainly hadn't been off the table!

* * *

Lee couldn't sit still for the rest of the evening, and her night's sleep was troubled by images of both Nathan and James. The reasons behind it were no mystery to Lee when she woke up tired and a bit irritable; she was nervous about the drink that evening and was clearly unsure about the decisions she was making.

The day passed in a blur with the usual routines and conversations that always made Lee's day different from the previous one. She tried (and failed) to avoid watching the clock, knowing that James would be meeting her once the shift ended. Gina saved her multiple times from making mistakes with orders because she just couldn't keep her mind focussed on one thing at a time. It was like she had too much energy and not enough all at once.

"Oh, just go and get changed, if you count that cash one more time I'm going to go crazy. I'll finish up here."

"You sure?" Lee asked, giving Gina an apologetic smile.

"Course. Go!"

Lee disappeared into the back room where she had stashed a change of clothes, a hair brush and some make up. Despite not wanting something serious, that didn't mean she was going to make no effort at all. Now that they had kissed - when she was covered in flour of all things - she was very keen to look as good as possible.

A quick flick of the hair brush, a change into black jeans and a festive sparkly top, a swish of eye shadow and Lee felt ready to take on the world. Well, for a drink with James anyway.

Gina wolf whistled as she exited into the now-empty café. "He'll want to bang your brains out too, looking like that!"

"Gina, you have got to stop using that phrase before someone overhears you!"

"You know I don't care. Have any amazing time, stay out late, don't be too loud if you come back to ours…"

"I'm sure I'll be back early, Gina! We're just going for a drink, and to talk, maybe another kiss… nothing more. Honest!"

"Mmhmm."

And then he was there, outside the door, shrouded in darkness under the spotlight of the Christmas decorations hung right outside the door. Lee didn't wait for him to come in; she opened the door and as the bell tinkled her face broke into a smile. He wore dark jeans and a plum coloured shirt that was open at the neck.

"Hey," Lee said, stepping out into the cold and feeling as though she was walking on air.

"Hey. You look fantastic, if you don't mind me saying."

"I don't mind at all. You scrub up pretty well too - although I'm rather partial to the police uniform, I have to say." She blushed and her hand flew to her mouth. "I'm sorry, I can't believe I just said that! I seem to struggle to think through my words when I'm around you."

James laughed and pulled Lee's hand down from her face. She felt tingles from every inch that he touched, and when he didn't let go of her hand, she didn't pull away either. "I'm glad you like the uniform," he said. "Shall we go get that drink? It's freezing here." He was beginning to think he should have worn his thick winter coat, but the idea just hadn't come into his mind as he was leaving the house for some reason.

"Lead the way," Lee said, and so he did, lacing his fingers between hers as he did so. It felt a little odd - she and Nathan hadn't, she realised, held hands in a long time - but it wasn't uncomfortable, and the tingling she felt where their bodies connected went some way to warming her on this cold December evening.

They entered a little bar halfway up the high street. The town was quaint in so many ways, and one was the fact that most of the shops that lined the steep hill were quite small; like Lee's café, they were intimate and only held a handful of customers - which had the added bonus and drawback (depending which side of the counter you were on!) of often being busy.

It was a weeknight, however, and so the little bar with its dark exposed beams and red feature wall only had a couple of other patrons in it. There was a little jazz music on in the background, but nothing loud enough to obscure talking - or a little flirting…

James didn't let go of her hand until they were sat at a mahogany table in the far corner of the room, beneath strings of fairy lights that made the place feel a little like a cosy cave. After asking what she wanted, James headed to the bar to grab drinks and

Lee allowed herself the luxury of a deep breath in as she reminded herself of the things she needed to say tonight - things that needed to be said before any more kissing was allowed to happen! She knew she needed to be up front and honest with him; he'd said she was brave, that she did what made her happy, and she thought some sort of involvement with James would make her happy - but she also knew that she was far too scared to get involved in anything serious. It was all too soon, and her wounded heart wasn't ready to be put through that wringer again.

She thought she'd got her heartbeat under control - and then he handed her a glass of wine, and his fingers brushed hers, and she was a mess of hormones all over again.

'Get a grip, Lee!' she told herself. '*You are not some fourteen-year-old with a crush.'*

Except that was exactly what she felt like.

"So," James said, taking a sip from his bottle of beer. "I know you like police uniforms-" Lee blushed and hoped it was hidden by the low light in the room. "That you make an amazing coffee and that you're clumsy with flour. What else? Where are you from?"

"Not normally so clumsy, thank you very much," Lee said with a grin. "I grew up just outside Bristol, and lived in Bristol up until last month. I went to university in London though - but I always planned to move back."

"You studied law in London then?"

"Yeah, and took the bar there too. I thought I'd stay there for a little while, but... well..." She trailed off, and took a large sip of wine to distract from that fact.

It didn't work.

"But?"

"Well, I probably shouldn't be talking about my soon-to-be ex-husband on this..." Again she trailed off; she had been about to say 'date', but wasn't sure if that was really the correct term for whatever this was.

"Drink," she finished, at the same time as James said "date". They both grinned.

"I asked the question - if you want to say it, I'll listen to the answer."

"Okay. Well, I met him when I was home visiting my mum and well - as they say, the rest is history. I moved back to Bristol not long after that, started working in a law firm and worked my way up to partner just as I hit thirty."

"Partner by thirty? Impressive," James said, raising his eyebrows slightly. "And a little intimidating!"

"Says you, PC Knight! What about you, how long have you been on the force?"

"Three years," James answered, running a hand through his slightly curly hair. "Finished school, had no idea what I wanted to do, did a bit of freelance art work for a bit and lived with my gran, then decided to sort myself out and get a degree. Went to university in Exeter, then got onto the police graduate program when I was twenty-five and here I am!"

"You're only twenty-eight?" Lee said, feeling ancient all of a sudden despite the difference only being a little over two years.

"Guilty as charged. And I would have said you were the same, except you just told me you became partner at thirty, so I must be wrong!"

She grinned a little at the flattery. "Thirty-one next month." She took a large gulp of wine and dived straight in to her own question. "So - and I'm just going to come out and say this - you've got a good job and you're gorgeous. How come you've not been snapped up?"

James tipped his head slightly to one side and shrugged a little. "Are you asking what's wrong with me?"

"No!" Lee said, almost spluttering out the sip of wine she'd taken. "Of course not!"

"Oh, I'm only joking. I guess I was - and then she decided she wanted to move to California to pursue life as a photographer out there, a week before our wedding. And, like an idiot, I offered to go with her - and realised that it wasn't just England she wanted to leave. It was me too. I heard she was in London recently - so maybe it was me more than England that she wanted to leave. There," he said, tapping the neck of his beer bottle onto the side of her glass of wine. "Now we've both shared too much about our exes for a date. Or a drink. Or whatever this is."

Lee looked down at the table and took a deep breath. "Is it a date?"

"I'd like it to be."

"I think I would too. But..."

"Always a but..." James said, but Lee was pleased to see he was grinning as he said it.

"I'm afraid so. I want it to be a date, and I'm trying to go for things I want. But I absolutely cannot commit to something serious right now - and I don't want to hurt you. And I don't want to lead you on."

James was silent for a few moments as he processed her words; she almost regretted saying them but she knew they needed to be said. However, just as strong within in her was a longing for that not to be the only kiss they ever shared…

"Okay," he suddenly said. "I think you're gorgeous, and you make me laugh, and I would really like to go on more than one date with you. So I'll take not serious for now - hey, you're moving back to Bristol at some point, that's bound to put a spanner in the works. And we'll both re-evaluate at a later date - how does that sound?"

"Sounds like a reason to kiss you," Lee said, with a cheeky grin that hid her own shock at her brazenness.

James didn't need asking twice. He leant across the table and their lips met; his hand moved to rest on the side of her head and - while the setting prevented them from being quite as enthusiastic as they had been in the store cupboard - Lee felt a slow burn start at her lips and spread to every inch of her body. She could taste the beer on his lips, and smell the faint scent of the aftershave she presumed he'd put on that evening. His face was certainly smooth; no hint of the stubble she had seen on him in previous days.

She had initiated it with her words and she broke it off, mindful that they were not the only ones in the cosy little bar. As they both gravitated back to the seats of their chairs, their faces were adorned with the widest grins and they found the conversation evaporated for a few moments as their gazes were locked.

"Definitely a good idea," James finally said.

"I'm full of them," Lee said with a smirk.

"I'd put visiting Totnes down as one of your better ones too," James said. "And wherever you went to make such a good cup of coffee."

"Can I tell you a secret?"

"Always."

"I had never made a proper cup of coffee - one that didn't come from a machine or a pot of granules - until I opened the café. Gina taught me everything she knew which - thank god - was a lot!"

"I never would have believed it. Best coffee I've ever tasted."

"I think you just enjoy flattering me," Lee said, but she was smiling.

"So," James said, finishing the end of his beer and rocking the bottle slightly on the table. "What's the plan, with 'Carol's Café'? Once you… if you move back to Bristol. And who is Carol anyway?"

"My gran," Lee said with a soft smile. "She passed away a long time ago, but she was always taking me to coffee shops and teaching me all the names of the coffees - and letting me order crazy flavoured milkshakes. Hey, I was eight! So I named it after her. Plus I love the alliteration."

"Both great reasons," James said; he fell silent as he waited for her to answer his initial question. She took the last sip of her wine for some kind of fortitude before answering.

"I decided to stay for Christmas, and I'll head back home - or wherever that ends up being - in the New Year. A fresh start. And then Gina will take over running, and I'll pay her and treat it as an investment, I guess." The idea sounded so strange, so detached; she couldn't imagine not running the café, not seeing the customers, not having a day to day say in the running of it. But she guessed that was what would happen, once she returned to some new flat in Bristol, back to her familiar life as a lawyer.

"New Year," James said. "That's not long…"

"No…" The unspoken words hung around them in the air as if they were being shouted. Were they crazy? Why were they starting anything, casual or not? They had a couple of weeks, tops. And then they would live two hours away from one another, with busy lives where whatever fling they decided to have would be long forgotten - a Christmas dream from another lifetime.

James reached across to gently trail his fingers across Lee's upturned palm and the realisation of 'why' shot through her like a bolt of lightning. This chemistry was not something to be ignored. She was not sure she'd ever felt a pull like this towards a man - and she didn't think it was something she could pass by, no matter how fleeting, no matter how disastrous the consequences would be.

She was glad when James opened his mouth, for she was sure she hadn't been too far off letting Gina's favourite phrase slip out; but she wasn't quite that daring.

"I can't have another, I need to drive," James said, and Lee felt her heart sink with disappointment. He hadn't felt the answer to the 'why?' coursing through his very veins then - he couldn't have done if he was ending this so early. She glanced at the clock; it wasn't even seven. She'd thought they might get some dinner, although her body couldn't possibly think about food with so many hormones filling it.

"Oh," she said, not sure what to respond; asking him to stay looked desperate, she felt - and besides, she'd been the one to say they couldn't date, she'd been the one to say it couldn't be serious - if he was now taking her at her word, she couldn't interfere. "Do you live far?" It wasn't what she wanted to say, but it was the only thing that she could think of to fill the silence.

"Just on the outskirts of Totnes - out towards the road to Kingsbridge, at the top of the hill. Not too far, but a bit too far to walk, especially at this time of year. And, as I'm sure you're aware by now, getting a taxi round here is often easier said than done."

She nodded; it was more something to plan in advance than a spur of the moment decision, that was true. "I guess you better get going."

"Do you - do you want to come back to mine for a drink? And I could fix us something to eat." He was fiddling with the label on his beer bottle, slowly shredding it off as he spoke to her; she wondered if it was out of nerves.

His words lifted her sinking spirits and she smiled broadly. "Yeah. That sounds good." She knew what she was getting herself into; she knew that if she was alone with him, and there was wine, what was likely to happen. And yet she followed him out of that bar, feeling touched by his thoughtfulness as he took her hand once more and led the way into the cold night air.

CHAPTER FOURTEEN

James was parked along the road a five minute walk from the bar, and as they walked with their hands joined together Lee commented on how beautiful the stars were above them. "They're so clear out here. It's never this clear back home - look, you can really see the constellations!" He laughed at her childish excitement, and began to point out the few constellations he could name, taking the hand that wasn't entwined with Lee's and using it to sketch them in the sky. Lee wasn't sure she would remember it all, but just hearing his deep, even voice talk with such knowledge, such confidence, kept her engrossed in every word.

It was only a short drive up the hill to James' house, and as they drove Lee felt butterflies begin to flutter in her stomach. Excitement? Or nerves? She wasn't sure, but she knew that going back to a man's house for a drink was something she hadn't done in years.

They turned off the main road down a small beaten pathway that Lee would have seen and dismissed as not being fit for cars. It widened slightly and then turned left into a small paved driveway with just enough room for one car. The engine stilled, and as they got out Lee looked around, her eyes trying to accommodate to the darkness. Here, slightly outside of the town, the stars were even brighter, and as the moon appeared from behind a cloud she saw that James' home was a little cottage, complete with a thatch roof and what looked like a white picket fence.

"This looks like a house from a fairy tale," she commented as she followed him inside.

"I know - not exactly what you imagine for a nearly thirty year old police officer, is it! But I love it." He opened the door and flicked the lights on; Lee's eyes blinked a little as they adjusted to the sudden glaring light, and she followed James through to a living room.

For all he said it wasn't the kind of home people imagined, when she stepped into the living room she could just feel his presence. There was a dark blue sofa in the middle of the room, pointing towards the television. A coffee table sat between the two, with a book of South Devon photography lying open on it and a mug - but other than that, the room was amazingly tidy. On the mantlepiece were three photographs - one of James as a teenager, with a boy and a girl who looked about the same age as him; one of James with a much older woman who Lee presumed was his gran, and one of James graduating with two adults who she thought must be his parents.

Underneath the photos lay a real fire, which James set about to lighting after telling Lee to make herself at home. She sat slightly awkwardly on the edge of the blue sofa, looking around and admiring the Christmas tree in the corner decorated in red, gold and silver decorations with a sparkling star sat right on top.

"Wine okay?" he asked, and Lee nodded. He disappeared through a different door than they had walked in and returned with a bottle of wine and two glasses. "Are you starving? I'm afraid I've not planned anything but I'm sure I've got something I can knock together."

"I'm all right for now, thanks," Lee said, feeling a little more overwhelmed than she'd expected by the change in setting from public to private and so much more intimate.

James sat next to her on the sofa - another change from being over a table from her - and poured them both generous glasses of wine.

"So," he said, leaning back against the arm and regarding Lee. "Can I ask another question?"

"One more won't hurt, I guess." Lee grabbed her glass of wine and tried to settle back a little into the cushions.

"Lee… it's an unusual female name. Is there any story there? Is it short for something?"

Lee sighed, and closed her eyes for a second. "You really want to know?"

"I wouldn't have asked otherwise!"

"Promise you won't laugh?"

"I'll try very hard not to."

"My mother named me Shirley. I hate it, I feel about 102 - so I've always shorted it to Lee. Only my mum still calls me Shirley."

She risked a sideways glance at James and saw that, while he was trying to cover a chuckle, he wasn't outright laughing.

"It could be worse. At least it does shorten! And Lee suits you. Honest."

"Hmmm. Shirley and Elizabeth, she called us - child cruelty, I tell you. Now James, that's a nice, normal name that everyone can spell and doesn't sound like it belongs to your great aunt."

"I should hope not! Although nice and normal sounds suspiciously like a euphemism for boring."

"I'm sure you're not boring," Lee said, and as their eyes met she swallowed at the intensity of his gaze. Heat pooled within her and she found she had forgotten what - if anything - she was going to say next.

Her gaze dropped to his lips, hovering inches above the wine glass, slightly damp from his drink.

"And you're nothing like my great aunt," James said with a chuckle. He placed his glass down on the table and Lee followed suit, subconsciously licking her lips. She could feel her body leaning towards his, and his was following like a magnet. James placed his hand on the side of her head, letting his fingers intertwine with her blonde locks for a moment, saying nothing, moving nothing but his fingers. Lee eyes fluttered closed as she drank in the sensations - the warmth of the real fireplace and the tingling in her mind that was not just from the wine, but from his proximity; she was drunk on him.

She felt, rather than saw, him move in closer, and she expected to feel his lips on hers any second; when she didn't, her eyes flicked open and she saw him, lips hovering millimetres in front of hers, and the corners were turned up in a grin.

"What?" Lee asked, shocked a little at how husky her voice sounded. She felt almost desperate to feel his lips on hers again; every inch of her burned sitting this close to him without touching him - except for that hand resting against her head.

"You're beautiful," he said, without any reservations, and if she weren't swimming in those bright blue eyes, Lee would have dipped her head in embarrassment at his compliment. "And last week I thought I would never get the chance to kiss you - so I'm just enjoying the moment."

Lee was speechless. She wasn't sure anyone had ever said anything so heartfelt, so romantic to her. She couldn't ruminate on it for long, however, because James pressed his lips to her neck, her earlobe, the soft skin behind her ear, her collarbone… everywhere but her lips. She couldn't control the groan that escaped her lips, couldn't focus on anything but him, him, him.

Her arms snaked around his neck, pulling him closer and trying to get his lips back to hers - and when they did she felt like she was losing all control, all reason, all thought. His arms moved down, down, under her legs to pull her roughly onto his lap, their lips never parting. As their tongues danced together, their bodies moved closer, and Lee found herself fumbling with the buttons on his shirt, keen to feel his warm skin beneath her hands.

His hands moved back to her hair, more roughly this time, both sides, combing through it and trying to pull her ever closer. Lee found herself twisting without really realising it, her legs wrapped round James' waist, her hands pressed to his taut muscles as his shirt flapped open between them.

And then James stood, his hands beneath her thighs, her legs still round his waist, and lay Lee down on the fluffy rug beside the fireplace. Their lips apart and breath ragged, Lee looked up at James who was hovering a little above her. He was close enough that she could feel the heat radiating from him, she could smell his aftershave, she could feel his breath on her cheek.

Lee could admire his muscles from this angle, as he held himself above her; he obviously kept himself in good shape (well, she guessed for his job he needed to) and those muscles were flexed before her.

"Is this going too fast?" James asked in a murmur as he kissed behind her ear.

"No…" Lee said, turning her head to kiss his lips. "No, I want this." And she did; she put all thoughts aside of betrayal, of Nathan, of whether this would lead to future happiness or heartbreak, and lived in the moment. She knew, beyond a shadow of a doubt, that in this moment she wanted him. Every part of him.

"So do I."

* * *

Lee lay lazily in James' arms in front of the fireplace, a nearby throw pulled over the top of them to keep out the night chill and protect a little modesty - although Lee wasn't sure it was so necessary now. Beneath the cover, they were both completely naked; Lee's head resting on James' muscled chest, which was covered in a light dusting of fair hair. She could feel his heart beating beneath her ear, as both of their breathing slowly began to return to its normal tempo. Neither could wipe the grins off their faces, no matter how tired they were, and for a while neither spoke, enjoying the warmth and ambiance of the firelight and basking in the afterglow of their lust for one another. James' fingertips stroked rhythmically up and down Lee's bare arm, and although the fire that had burned through her had cooled down to embers for now, that simple contact felt as though it could slowly reignite it all over again.

"I'm loving this moment in time," James admitted, pressing his lips into the mess of her hair as he spoke.

"Me too," Lee said, and she knew the words were honest. In the short period she'd known him, Lee thought she'd only ever been honest with James - sometimes too honest, but she had never held back the truth. The buzz of thoughts that had been bombarding her head for months seemed to calm in this moment; she thought of nothing but his smooth, solid body beneath her, the rhythm of his breathing and the warmth of the fire.

And then her stomach rumbled.

Her hand dropped to it in embarrassment, but James just laughed. "I did promise you dinner…" he said with a grin.

"Lured me here under false pretences," Lee said, leaning her cheek against his shoulder. "And there was no police uniform in sight…"

"I can wear it next time, if you like!" Lee felt a warm, fuzzy feeling in her stomach at the thought of a 'next time'. Months and months without regular sex with Nathan and yet here and now she felt like her whole body ached for James; like there was something within her that only he could satisfy. In her logical mind, she knew that this was just the beginning of something new - as Gina had said, those first kisses, the potential awkwardness, the rush every time you touched… that was all part of the fun and excitement of a new relationship. But a voice in the back of Lee's head wondered if there was anything more to it; if there was something particularly explosive in the chemistry between her and James.

Her mind's ramblings were interrupted by James' voice. "Clearly you can't focus when you're hungry. I'll go put something on - it's gone nine already!" He stood, kindly leaving Lee the cover but exposing himself completely to her and the elements. He didn't seem overly concerned, grabbing his boxers from where they had ended up a metre away on the floor and quickly pulling on his trousers. He left the top off, leaving Lee to admire the sculpted muscles of his abdomen - surreptitiously, of course. In a very thoughtful gesture, he passed Lee her underwear before leaving the room, and she was grateful to be able to slip it back on without him watching. She didn't feel quite as comfortable in her naked skin as he clearly did - despite him murmuring admirations for it for the last hour or so.

Once she was wearing the matching black pants and bra again she had a flash of an idea, and decided to act upon it before her natural reticence overcame her. This bravery she felt in James' presence could be a dangerous thing…

He walked back in five minutes later, still bare chested despite the November chill, and Lee was sure she saw his mouth drop open slightly when he saw her.

Instead of dressing fully, she had taken his plum coloured shirt and put it on over her black underwear, buttoning it up part way but leaving two or three buttons open at the top, so her cleavage was quite visible. Added to the fact that it wasn't long enough to completely cover her bum… well, she felt his silence was the effect she had been hoping for, and grinned.

"You'll be lucky if I manage to make dinner at all this week, let alone tonight if you sit there in my shirt looking like *that*…"

Lee grinned and tried to look innocent. "I don't know what you mean, officer."

The words sent a slight jolt of want through both of them.

As it happened, they did manage to get some dinner - but only because, as they found themselves laying down on their sofa with their lips pressed together, James' stomach rumbled too. It seemed like it was best to put *that* on the back burner for long enough to eat dinner.

James had made a simple pasta dish, and Lee didn't know if he was an amazing cook or if she were just starving, but it was the best dish she'd ever eaten. They sat at a breakfast bar in the middle of a stone-walled kitchen, kept warm by an old fashioned looking Aga.

"I love this place," Lee said, looking around the kitchen while they ate. "It seems so homey, everywhere you look."

"Thanks. I love it too. It was my gran's - I have to admit that I haven't changed an awful lot from how she had it. Bought slightly less floral bedding, added a pot plant - but the essence of the place is still the same."

Lee remembered him talking about living with his gran for a while, back before he made the decision to become a police officer. "Did you live here with her?"

He nodded, a slightly sad smile on his lips. "Yes, until I went to uni - and then she died while I was there, although I got to come back in time, thank god."

"I'm sorry," she said, knowing the pain of a losing a grandparent in a way that she knew not everyone understood. To some they were a distant relative wheeled out at Christmases and birthdays. To Lee - and it seemed to James, too - they had been an integral part of her life.

"Thanks. She left me this place - knew I loved it. I love the memories here, as well as the building."

"What a great legacy," Lee said.

"As is your café, to your gran." She was touched that he had listened to those intimate details.

They were quiet for a few moments, enjoying their pasta and wine in a companionable silence. The clock ticked away above them and Lee was shocked when she noticed it was almost ten o'clock.

"What will you do for Christmas?" James asked casually, and Lee thought it might have been the first time in her adult life that she didn't have concrete plans for her favourite holiday.

"Probably just stay in, spend some time with Gina before she goes to her family, drink a bottle of wine and watch Christmas films!" she said. "I'm not in the mood to spend it with my family, all those reminders of a past I want to forget. I'm sure they won't mind too much." She wasn't sure at all, in fact, but she knew she couldn't go to her mum's house where her and Nathan's wedding photos were proudly displayed, where she had spent so many Christmases with mum, Beth and Nathan. It was too painful, too raw; maybe next year it wouldn't be.

"I get that. I don't like to think of you on your own though..."

"I'll be fine. What do you do Christmas day then?" she asked, trying to take the attention off her Christmas which did, even to her ears, sound a bit like a pity party. Belatedly, she realised he might take it as a hint for an invite, which it most definitely was not - Christmas day with someone did not constitute 'no commitment' and 'taking things slow' by any means. But it was too late to take it back.

"For the last couple of years I've had the whole family round here," James said. "I worked the year after gran died, and got called in the year after, but we've done two Christmases here. They all say this place has the most Christmas spirit, not to mention the most room - and since I'm the one who enjoys this time of year the most, I host."

"Who's all the family?" Lee asked, always intrigued by big families since she herself had come from such a compact one.

"Mum, dad, brother, sister and two sister-in-laws - my brother's wife and my sister's wife."

"Sounds busy. And you cook for them all?" She was thinking, however inappropriately, back to Nathan; she couldn't imagine him ever cooking Christmas dinner, let alone for the whole family. That was why their diet had consisted so often of takeaways...

"I try my best!" he said with a laugh. "I'm no master chef but I do okay," he said. "Mum helps out," he added with a fond grin.

They finished dinner and James declined Lee's offer to wash up, insisting it could wait 'til morning. Lee glanced at the clock; already ten thirty five.

"I should get going," Lee said; "I've got an early start."

James looked disappointed. They were stood opposite one another, James a little taller than Lee despite her height. He'd thrown a t-shirt on to ward off the cold; she was still dressed in only her underwear and his shirt, and was beginning to shiver a little.

"Stay," James said, reaching out and taking her hand. "I'd really like you to stay the night."

"James..." she said, with more longing in her voice than she had intended. "We said something casual... no commitment. I feel like staying is mixing all those signals, crossing all those wires..."

"It's not. Lee, I know you can't commit right now. I know I'm likely to end up with a broken heart at the end of all this - no, don't look shocked, I want you to know that I'm very much hoping you'll eventually change your mind and want something more serious. But right now you can't, and that's fine. And if you never do, I promise I won't hold it against you. But it's late..." He took a step closer. "And it's cold..." Another step, their chests were touching and Lee found she had to tilt her neck to meet those piercing blue eyes. "And I want you."

Those words... those words were enough to make her throw caution to the wind, to ignore all the barriers she had tried to put in place around this handsome man and press her lips furiously against his.

"Is that a yes?"

"I don't have a toothbrush..."

"I've got a spare."

"I don't have pyjamas…"

"You won't need them…"

Lee grinned naughtily. "Okay. Okay…"

James cheered and lifted her off her feet; she giggled, feeling amazingly free and easy as she wrapped her legs around his waist.

"I better find my police hat…" he said, and Lee threw her head back in laughter.

* * *

An hour later, with James softly snoring next to her under his dark blue duvet cover, Lee reached out of the bed to find her phone. She wasn't surprised to see two texts from Gina.

Hope things are going well - I expect details! G xxx

Where are you, dirty stop out?! Let me know you're okay. I'll open up tomorrow - come in whenever you're ready.

Lee grinned in the darkness at that; it was exactly what she had been hoping for. She quickly fired off a text to Gina before James' hand reached out and pulled her back under the covers, wrapping his body around hers until her naked back was pressed to his naked chest, and his arm was wrapped around her waist. Lee let her eyes flutter closed as she relaxed into him, letting his deep breaths lull her to sleep.

A mile or so away, Gina grinned sleepily at the message she received.

Thanks, I owe you one! Won't be back tonight I'm afraid ;) But I'm fine! xxx

CHAPTER FIFTEEN

The next day, Lee woke up with a start at nine am - quite a lot later than she normally woke up - and took a second or two to remember where she was. In the winter morning light, the exposed beams were highlighted and the frost on the windows made the light dance in mesmerising patterns on the wall. The air in the room was chilly, but the body next to her was oh so warm that, without even thinking, she cuddled up in order to keep the iciness from chilling her.

James looked just as gorgeous in the morning light as he had done the night before; hair slightly tousled, mouth slightly open, and with a hint of stubble on his chin. She watched him sleep for a few moments, before laying her head back down on his chest and contemplating her actions,

It had been six years since she had last slept with somebody other than Nathan. Her count wasn't particularly high; there had been a fling in university, then a long term boyfriend in law school and then Nathan. Three - which had now become four. Did she regret it? She couldn't bring herself to. Both times had been utterly electric - a chemistry she couldn't remember ever feeling with the others. And she had been very clear; she could not commit right now. So she didn't have to worry about hurting anyone - although she thought, somewhere in the back of her head where the little reasonable voice spoke, that she might be lying to herself there. That there were two people who were very much in danger of getting hurt…

James stirred then, wrapping his arm tightly around her as he stretched out his legs, his toes poking out from under the duvet at the end of the bed.

"Morning," James said, as Lee tilted her head to look up at him. For a second she worried about how she must look after a night of passionate sex. Perhaps the time watching him sleeping would have been better spent combing her hair and brushing her teeth…

But it was too late for that now. And as his lips pressed onto hers in a sweet, languishing kiss, she found she stopped caring. Her back arched as her fingers tugged at his hair, and his arms snaked around her, pulling her closer to him as their tongues met.

"Good morning," Lee said eventually, her breathing not as calm as it had been before their lips had met.

"What time is it?" asked James.

"About nine-thirty, I think."

"I thought you had an early start."

"I did… but Gina offered to open up."

"So you can stay in bed while I make love to you all day?" James asked. His body covered hers and he pressed his lips into the curve of her neck, the crevice of her collar bone, between her breasts…

Lee giggled a little and wriggled her hips as she felt the desire building in her again. "Well, maybe not all day… she said to go in when I was ready."

"That may not be for a few hours, because you're naked in my bed and I don't see any reason for us to change that situation…"

* * *

An hour later, and after a steamy shower together (that probably took twice as long as individual showers would have taken), Lee decided that she really should be getting to work.

"It's not fair on Gina," Lee said for the fifth time as James tried to persuade her to stay for lunch. "And I have a feeling that lunch will turn into us heading back upstairs, and then having dinner… and I'll never make it to work."

"That might not happen," James said with a smile.

"Oh, I think it will."

"Okay, okay. Can I take you out again?"

"I'd love that," Lee said with a smile. She was a little self-conscious of the fact that she was wearing yesterday's creased clothes (that had been picked up off the living room floor that morning), and that she'd had to use James' comb to try to get her hair to become manageable again.

"How about tomorrow afternoon? I've got an idea…"

"I'll check my calendar - but that sounds like a plan."

They drove down the hill and through the town, listening to Christmas tunes on the radio and laughing about the lyrics. Luckily, James found a spot to pull up right outside the café, and so Lee didn't have to brave the rain.

"Thank you," she said, un-clipping her seatbelt and lifting her handbag from the floor.

"For the lift?"

"For the lift… and the amazing night."

“It was my pleasure. Literally…” He said with a cheeky grin. “It was a mind-blowingly brilliant night. Thank *you*. And I can’t wait to take you out again.” He leant over and kissed her cheek; a soft, gentle kiss that nevertheless set her blood racing and her cheeks aflame.

“See you tomorrow, Lee.”

“See you tomorrow James.”

She watched as he drove off, wasting that close parking space by standing out in the rain for longer than was sensible. She felt as though she was walking on air, skating through the doorway with the most ridiculously big smile on her face.

The café was heaving when she finally came back to down to earth for long enough to realise; every table was full and there was a queue at the counter.

“Sorry!” Lee said, rushing behind the counter and tying an apron on quickly. “Sorry, sorry, sorry!”

“No worries,” Gina said, passing her three orders to make. “But I’m glad to see you! And I want all the details once we get through this rush.”

Lee blushed, and nodded. “Okay. All the details…”

It was gone four o’clock before things even calmed down a little - their new kids’ hot chocolates seemed to be going down very well with all the children on their holidays, and the parents were generally persuaded into a coffee and a cake as well. All in all, very good for business - but not so good for sharing the juicy details of Lee’s night. It wasn’t until they were closing up that they had any chance to share more than orders - but the second the door was locked behind the last customer, Gina wheeled round to face her with a big grin on her face.

"You sweep, I'll mop, you give me the details. Agreed?"

"Oh, go on then," Lee said with a laugh. She grabbed the broom from behind the counter, and waited for Gina to fill the mop bucket with boiling water before talking.

"So, as I'm sure you guessed, our drink went well."

"Where did you go?"

"That little place, just up the road - The Bear, I think it's called? We went, had a drink, flirted, kissed…"

"Oh, quick mover then!"

"And then he asked if I wanted to go back to his for a drink…"

Gina wiggled her eyebrows. "Which you obviously said no to and came straight back home for an early night."

"Oh, of course." Lee laughed; Gina began to follow the path she had swept with the steaming water from the mop. "I told him, though. I told him I can't commit right now, that it's too soon after Nathan, that I don't know where my life is going…"

"And?"

"And he said that while it wasn't what he'd choose, he was happy with it for now and he understood. And then we went back to his…

"Does he live far?"

"No, just up over the hill towards Kingsbridge, in the most gorgeous little cottage. There was a real fire, he cooked me pasta…"

"And he banged your brains out?!"

"Once or twice!" Lee said, her grin accompanied by a blush.

"Get you - it's always the quiet ones! Didn't I say it was a good idea to talk to him about it, rather than just write him off? So, you had a good night."

"I'm so confused by all of this but, yes, yes I had a great night. And a great morning, and he wants to take me out again tomorrow night…"

"What's there to be confused about?" Gina asked, finishing the mopping only moments after Lee had finished sweeping. "You've got electric chemistry, you flirt whenever you're around him, you've had amazing sex with him - at least, I presume it was amazing from that grin on your face - and he's okay with the fact that you just can't look at the long term at the minute." Lee began to cash up and Gina emptied the now dirty water down the sink. "I say you enjoy it and see how it goes. Don't stress about the future - it's always been my philosophy, and things are going all right for me!"

It wasn't until they were walking down to where Lee had left the car the day before that she thought to check her phone. Two messages popped up on the screen.

I hope you weren't too tired at work. Thanks for a wonderful night - until tomorrow! James x

That one made her grin, and she planned to think of a response on the drive home. The next one, however, sent her brain back into the disarray it seemed to have been in for the last month.

Just checking, we'll definitely be seeing you when we open January 2nd? We miss you and we're crazily busy! Tania and Gemma xxx

January 2nd… that was the day she'd said she would return to work. Start a new year and then back, back to the office, back to real life. Less than two weeks away…

As she contemplated the fact that she was leaving Totnes - and the café, and Gina, and James - in under two weeks, she felt the smile dissolve from her face. Life felt even more complicated than before.

CHAPTER SIXTEEN

James was waiting outside in his car the following day when Lee had locked up. She wasn't sure where they were going, so she'd quickly changed out of her work gear in the back room and put on some black jeans and a smart, green knitted jumper that she had borrowed from Gina. On Gina's suggestion, she had also thrown a spare toothbrush and a fresh pair of knickers in her handbag - well, Gina insisted that it was always good to be prepared, and Lee thought it wasn't the worst idea she'd ever heard.

He threw the door open as she stepped out onto the pavement, and she gratefully climbed in to the front seat of the warm car.

"Good evening," he said with a smile, and she laughed as she saw he was wearing his police officer hat with his jeans and polo shirt.

"Good evening," she said, and James leaned over to kiss her, his lips lingering just a fraction longer than was necessary in a greeting, his hand placed lightly on her waist. He took off the hat and placed it on her head, then laughed and pulled away from the café.

"How come you're wearing this?" she asked, removing the hat and turning it over in her hands.

"You said you liked the uniform, and I was worried you hadn't seen me in it in a while…"

"Nice touch," Lee said. "You do seem to have been off work for a couple of days!"

"I'd been on ten days straight before, so I've got four days off now. Then back in tomorrow - I've managed to get Christmas day off though, which is nice."

"Ah, and here I thought you were skiving just to spend time with me," Lee said with a grin.

"I would," James said, and although there was a smile on his face he didn't laugh.

"So," Lee asked, "Where are we going?"

"Ahh, you'll see. Somewhere to keep that festive spirit alive… after all, it is only five days until Christmas!"

"Five days… I feel like the last six weeks have just disappeared. I can't believe we're that close to Christmas…"

"They're saying it's the best chance of having a white Christmas in years!" James said, tapping on the temperature reading on the display. "Certainly cold enough for it."

"Do you think it will? I can't remember the last time it snowed on Christmas day."

"Don't get your hopes up," James said with a smile. "It never snows this near to the coast." They were leaving now, heading on the dual carriageway. As the speedometer began to rise on the largely empty road, Lee turned up the Christmas songs on the radio and soaked up the festive spirit.

*   *   *

They pulled up outside a large garden centre, covered in lights and open despite it being six o'clock. Lee couldn't help but feel a little confused as they parked and she glanced out into the dark night sky to see why they might be here.

"Right this way," James said, noticing her quizzical looks but not answering them - yet. He took her hand and Lee was amazed how natural it felt, walking in the cool night air, hand in hand with this tall, fair police officer. Both had coats and scarves pulled tightly around themselves, and as they approached the crooning of Frank Sinatra could be heard from speakers just inside the door.

They stepped into a winter wonderland. The entrance was filled with fake snow - on the floor, falling from the ceiling, around the feet of the amazed children running all about. To each side were snowy scenes; a large model polar bear alongside a deer; and on the other side, Santa in his sleigh filled to bursting with presents. Lee couldn't take her eyes off the magical displays.

"What is this place?" Lee asked, eyes wide.

"It's a garden centre, like it looks," James explained, leading Lee in through to main shop. "But they do the most amazing Christmas displays, and tonight they're staying open late with hot chocolate, and mince pies, and carolling…" He glanced at her sideways, looking to see how she was taking this choice of venue.

"I know it's a bit of an odd choice for a date, but I thought-"

"It's wonderful, James," Lee said, and she turned and planted a kiss on his cheek. "Come on, there's so much to see!" James laughed at her excitement, her impatience, and together they ducked under an archway covered in holly and entered the festive magic.

Magical scenes from fairy tales, staff dressed as elves, a Santa's grotto and some of the most beautiful ornaments Lee had ever seen awaited them inside. Lee gasped at so many things that night, and James grinned at how much pleasure she took from every little detail. And as they walked they talked; a beautiful glass ballerina ornament started off a story from when Lee had been in ballet classes up until the age of seven - lessons that had never gone particularly well since Lee had always been tall for her age and lacking in co-ordination. A handsome felted black Labrador ornament led James to talk about his childhood dog, Mikey, and the adventures they'd had on the beaches of Devon.

Eventually they sat to drink hot chocolates and eat mince pies on tables lit by candlelight with the background of carollers singing Christmas classics.

"What a lovely evening, James - I don't think I've felt this festive all month. Thank you."

"I love seeing how excited you get - makes the Christmas magic feel all the more special."

They clinked mugs and sipped the creamy hot chocolate. "Can I ask you a sensitive question?" James asked, just as Lee had bitten into a mince pie and was focusing on not having crumbs and icing sugar across her lips. She nodded, intrigued.

"How long were you married for?"

It wasn't what she'd been expecting, and not a topic she particularly wanted to discuss - but she guessed she couldn't blame him for being curious. "Five years," she said once her mouth was empty. "Together for six. Although now I feel like I never really knew him at all."

"What's he called?"

"Nathan. Nathan Jones… that's why I've gone back to my maiden name. I feel like I didn't know him, didn't really know myself during that time. It's put a whole difference perspective on the last few years of my life. It doesn't quite feel real…"

"I bet," James said, taking hold of her hand across the table. "I know it was longer ago, but I felt the same when - when Sofia left me. And now I can look back and see that my life is so much better now than it was then. You will find your bearings, and it will be better than before. I'm sure of it."

Lee was embarrassed to realise that there were tears pooling in her eyes. "Thank you. That does make me feel a bit better about it all. And," she blinked to clear the tears that luckily had not been shed, "I'm very, very happy right now. Tonight feels truly magical."

They wandered happily through the last few displays that they had missed, and reached a Christmas photo booth with a small queue.

"Shall we?" Lee asked, a smile on her face, fairly sure that James would not deny her this.

"After you," he said. The queue disappeared quickly and then they stepped through the curtain where there was a screen, a few props and a bench. Santa hats and beards, candy canes and elf ears were all there, and Lee grabbed a green elf hat with a jingling bell on the end and pushed it onto her head; James chose a red Santa hat tipped with white fur.

"Right, I'll press the button, you make sure you look gorgeous," James said with a wink, and he reached forward to press it before leaning back and putting his arm round Lee. For the first they smiled; the camera counted down and James pressed a kiss to Lee's cheek; as it counted down the third time neither saw it reach zero, for their lips were on each other's, and it was more than just a gentle kiss.

"Thank you for using the Christmas photo booth!" a voice called out from the machine, causing them to jump and disengage from one another. The three photos appeared on the screen, with a choice of backgrounds - snow, glitter, or Christmas trees. Lee took the lead, pressing buttons until the three photos had a different background each and pressed print. As she exited, James pressed the button again.

"Oh, it's printed two!" Lee said as she collected them.

"I presumed the first lot were for you, and I wanted a copy!"

"I was going to share," Lee said, sticking out her tongue and glancing at the copies. Her favourite was the one where James had kissed her cheek. She was flushed, smiling, ecstatic looking; and despite kissing her, you could see the upturned lips peeking out from where they met her skin. She loved the looks of happiness on their faces.

Placing the photos in her bag carefully, she glanced up and her smile widened. James' glance followed hers: mistletoe.

"Well, we may have jumped the gun slightly on that one," Lee said with a little laugh.

"But we can't ignore mistletoe Lee, it's the rules…" For a moment their eyes met and neither moved a muscle, caught in the moment with the Christmas music and fake snow all around them. Then their lips touched and they allowed themselves the luxury of a few seconds of kissing in this crowded place - after all, there was mistletoe. And it was part of the Christmas rules…

"Right, I need to run to the ladies quickly, okay?" Lee said.

"I'll meet you by the door then, okay? We'll go and get some dinner, if that sounds good."

"Brilliant."

Lee wound her way back through the festive maze of decorations, but not towards the signs for the bathrooms. She struggled to find her way back, and was beginning to stress about the time she had been gone, when she spotted it. She headed straight for the tills and got it into her bag as quickly as possible, so James wouldn't see it.

It had been a spur of the moment decision, and never had they said they would get each other Christmas gifts, but Lee knew she couldn't leave the shop without that black Labrador ornament.

James was waiting by the door, slightly taller than the majority of the other shoppers, and Lee made a beeline for him. Without saying anything, he held out his hand and she slipped hers into his as if it were the most natural thing in the world.

"Ready for dinner?" he asked, and she nodded; it was great to be out with him, and it was great to see more of the area than just Totnes and Dartmouth, the only two places she had really visited.

"Could we go to a beach?" she asked as they were driving. "Before I go, I mean? I realised I've been in Devon a month and not been to a beach - even in the winter that's got to be some sort of crime, right?"

"Definitely," James said with a grin. "We could go on the twenty-seventh? If you don't have to work."

"I'm sure I can square it," Lee said, excited that they had planned another date.

They pulled up outside a small village pub, with a Christmas tree out in front and red lights strung in all the windows. The huge wooden door opened into a cosy pub with a roaring fire and yet another beautifully decorated Christmas tree, surrounded by presents that Lee assumed were props.

"This okay?" James asked, running his hand through his hair.

"Looks great. Can I get you a drink?"

"I'll get them," James said, putting his hand in his pocket to pull out his wallet.

"No, you've cooked for me and bought me hot chocolate and mince pies - I'll get these."

"If you're sure - I brought you here, I'm happy to pay!"

"No, honestly."

"All right, all right, you've twisted my arm. I'll have a half pint of whatever's on tap please," James said.

They took their drinks and two menus to a table nearest the fire, and Lee was pleased to be able to defrost a little and remove her coat. They ordered fish and chips - it seemed like a very appropriate menu for the location, if not the weather - and were chatting away as they waited for it to come.

"So," James asked, sipping his beer and regarding her over the top of it. "You're nearly at the end of your stay in Totnes. How's it been?"

"Exactly what I needed," Lee said, without missing a beat. "I mean, Totnes is so different to anywhere I've been before… and some of the people I've met have been a bit unusual - did I tell you about the time I tried to get a bus and a man tried to sell me a book on the occult? He would not take no for an answer, I had to get off at the next stop." Lee laughed at the memory, which had given her a very interesting flavour of a few of the town's residents. "But I've loved it."

"Can I ask, then," James began, swallowing before he continued. "Why you're leaving?"

"James…" It was such a hard question, and it felt so much like her leaving was linked to him, like leaving was akin to saying that she didn't want a relationship with him - but it had always been in the plan, to leave. She was a lawyer, a partner - she couldn't leave that forever. This was always going to be a break, not her new life.

Wasn't it?

"I'm not pressuring you, and it's not about us, I promise. Well, it's not totally about us. But… you said yourself, you've loved it. And so I just don't understand why you don't make it permanent, if you're happy."

Lee was given a brief moment of respite as their food was set down on the table in front of them, and she tried to put all the thoughts and feelings into words.

"I am happy. These last few days with you… this last month with Gina, and the café - it's given me more happiness than I've felt in a long time. But maybe that's because it's all new; and I do have a life up there. Granted, I don't have a home, or a husband anymore - and I have a divorce to organise. But I have a career, and I worked too hard on that to give up on it."

She was becoming upset now; she had let herself forget that when she went back it wouldn't just be to her job, but to trying to find a home, to no husband, to divorce papers and arguments over money. While she was here, Nathan seemed to have generally left her alone…

James' hand reached hers across the table. "I'm sorry, Lee. I shouldn't have pushed it. It's just… you seem happy, and I want you to keep having that. But now I'm the idiot who's made you unhappy. Let's just forget it, hey, and enjoy the rest of the days we've got together? Because these last two dates have been the most fun I've had in years."

Lee smiled a little, and squeezed his hand before reaching for her knife and fork. As they ate, his words swirled around her head, making her question the decisions she had made. It all seemed so obvious: she had a job to get back to, she needed to return.

But was that completely necessary?

CHAPTER SEVENTEEN

Christmas day dawned cold and bright, but without the promised snow. Lee woke up at nine, relishing the chance for a lie-in with the café closed and no pressures on her for the day. She lay in bed for half an hour, letting herself wallow a little; allowing herself to think about what this day would normally hold.

She would have been up early wrapping last minute presents - she was always too busy before Christmas to get it done in time - and would enjoy a glass of bubbly with Nathan to celebrate the festive day. She found it wasn't as painful to think of Nathan a few weeks on… but it was still painful to think of what could have been.

Then they would drive to her mother's house, laden with gifts and the traditional fruit cake that Lee always brought to Christmas dinner. Beth would be there, complaining about the commercialism and stealing Christmas cookies when she thought she could get away with it without her mother telling her off for ruining her appetite.

And they would have the big meal together, just the four of them (unless Beth had happened to have a boyfriend that year) and watch the Queen's speech on the television. Then Nathan would usually fall asleep in the chair after one too many glasses of wine, and Lee would have to avoid the alcohol because she was the designated driver. Mum, Beth and Lee would share a box of chocolates, watch a Christmas film and for once feel as though they were on exactly the same page.

The one thing that Lee had wanted for the last couple of years was children around, to make the day more magical; children to wrap presents for, children waking her up early in the morning to see if Father Christmas had been.

But that was a dream that belonged in the past, she decided; it wasn't realistic right now. And so she tried to push it from her mind and focus on what was going to be great about this Christmas day. She was spending the morning with Gina (who she presumed was still sleeping off a hangover from her Christmas Eve night out with friends the night before, which Lee had politely declined going to), and they were going to watch a Christmas film and drink Buck's Fizz together. Then Gina would go off to her parents' house, and Lee planned to have a soak in the bath, cook her own Christmas dinner for the first time ever and then sit in front of Christmas TV for the afternoon - alongside a bottle of wine or two. There was a festive novel waiting for her on the bookcase if she decided she'd had enough of TV for the day.

She left the warmth of her bedroom for the living room once she'd decided enough wallowing in the past was enough, and clicked the kettle on for a cup of coffee before the Buck's Fizz. The heating clicked on and Lee found something suitably festive on the television and immediately began singing along to the Christmas tunes.

Gina appeared soon after: her hair was a little bedraggled and she had a slightly sore head, but she smiled when she saw Lee caught up in the festive spirit.

"Merry Christmas!" Lee said as she spotted her friend and flatmate enter the room. "Coffee's ready for you!"

"Merry Christmas - even if no-one should be this chirpy at this time of the morning."

"I've decided to take every ounce of Christmas joy I can find, and leave any negativity at the door."

"Sounds like a plan," Gina said, hopping over the back of the sofa, grabbing her coffee from the side where Lee had left it.

“And I’m looking forward to my very first Christmas dinner cooked by me. I don’t know how I’ve got through so many years without getting round to cooking one.”

“Ah, I haven’t either - I just always go to my mum’s! Are you sure you’re going to be all right here on your own? I feel awful leaving you.”

“Don’t be silly, I’ll be fine. I’m looking forward to it.”

“You could always go round to James’… you have a Christmas gift for him, don’t you?”

“He never invited me for Christmas, G - I can’t exactly turn up. Besides, that says a lot more commitment than I can handle, when I’m leaving in a few days.”

“I still can’t believe I’m going to have to find a new flatmate,” Gina said with a sigh.

“No negativity on Christmas day!” Lee said. “But you know I’m sorry. And I’ve paid the rent for two months, so there’s no rush. Besides, hopefully the café will bring in enough that you won’t need to have a flatmate eventually.”

“Yeah, yeah,” Gina said, rolling her eyes with a good-natured smile.

Lee popped the cork to the bubbly and quickly poured it into two glasses before it fizzed over. She handed one to Gina, and they clinked their glasses together. “To Christmas wishes,” Gina said with a grin. “May they all come true.”

“I’ll drink to that,” Lee said, settling down on the sofa with a blanket over her legs.

"Hey, Lee, look! Look! It's snowing!" Lee turned her head towards the window, and sure enough, small little white flakes were falling from the sky. They both jumped up, as excited as school kids, and pressed their faces to the window to see the first white Christmas either of them could remember. The flakes weren't massive, it was true, and they weren't falling that fast - but they were beginning to settle on the abandoned pavements outside their flat and on the rooftops of houses filled with Christmas lights.

At that moment, Lee's phone buzzed in her pyjama pocket, and she pulled it out to find a message from James.

It looks like the Christmas wish of a white Christmas did come true! Here's hoping both of our Christmas wishes come true. Merry Christmas Lee - looking forward to our beach visit. James xxx

Gina, who was reading over her shoulder, chuckled and gave Lee a friendly shove. "You should so go over there. Surprise him. Maybe wearing a coat and nothing underneath…"

"Gina!" Lee shrieked. "As if I could do that! And stop reading my messages."

"Yeah, yeah, you totally could, but maybe it's more my style than yours. Anyway, it's present time." She bent below their Christmas tree, decorated in lights, tinsel and baubles of every shape, colour and size, and passed Lee a flat, rectangular present wrapped in sparkly blue paper.

"Gina, you didn't need to get me anything!"

"Open it, open it!" she said, the Christmas excitement having clearly affected her.

Lee ripped the paper off eagerly, and found a beautiful print in a thin, silver frame. The print was an artistic portrayal of Totnes high street, with snow covering the buildings and the roads.

"I thought it could go in your office in Bristol," Gina said with a sad smile. "And remind you of us - and make sure you visit the café you own!"

Lee threw her arms around Gina, desperate to hide the tears that she could feel beginning to fall. "It's perfect, Gina - and I'll definitely be back. You'll be wishing you could get rid of me."

"Oh," said Gina, trying to ignore the fact that they both had tears in their eyes. "You're not going to become that boss, are you - the one that never lets the manager just get on with her job?"

Lee laughed; "That sounds just like me! Now, my turn." She pulled a second parcel from under the tree. This one was wrapped in silver paper, and it was small and hard. Gina ripped the paper off as enthusiastically as Lee had, and looked a little surprised to see a blue jewellery box. She lifted the lid cautiously, and there lay a pair of delicate silver unicorns, hanging from earrings. Their horns were tiny coloured gems and a light sparkle shimmered on their tails.

"I thought they were unique, just like you," Lee said.

"I love them! Thanks, Lee." They hugged again, admiring their presents in the strange light coming through the snow-covered window.

"Come on then, this Christmas film won't watch itself," Gina said, and they both tried to put their presents and their emotions to one side, and enjoy a festive-filled couple of hours.

It felt like no time at all until Gina had to go, and Lee realised that she had been so wrapped up in their film and the snow that she hadn't replied to James' text. She glanced out of the window, where all the houses and streets looked like they were covered in a light dusting of icing sugar, before pulling out her phone.

Merry Christmas! Definitely feels like a bit of Christmas magic. See you the day after tomorrow - unless we're snowed in! :) Lee xxx

She glanced at the small, silver parcel sat under the tree for James, and wondered whether it had been a silly idea - would it be too late to give it to him on the twenty-seventh? She realised she really should have given it to him before Christmas - but something had been holding her back. Maybe she hadn't wanted to seem like she was building any sort of long lasting relationship with him… because it had been her who had said she couldn't commit.

Bringing her phone into the bathroom to blast out some Christmas music, Lee ran a boiling hot bath with plenty of bubbles and a sprinkle of the bath salts she had treated herself to the previous week. She watched as the bubbles grew, filling the bath, crackling quietly as they began to pop. The frosted glass that looked out onto the street always let in limited light, but with a dusting of snow building up on it the room grew even darker, and so Lee decided to light some candles.

Excited about her luxurious Christmas bath, she stripped off and quickly slid under the hot water and bubbles as - even with the heating having been on all day - the air in the flat was chilly. She swirled her hand through the bubbly water, enjoying the feeling of the water on her cold skin, feeling her muscles relaxing after a very busy week in the café.

It was here that - despite the loud Christmas music - she let her mind wander. She closed her eyes and pictured James, and found herself smiling. He'd asked her why she couldn't stay - now she found herself asking the same question. Yes, the law firm, yes, her job… but god he made her happy. She knew it was new and exciting and the chemistry was electric… but she was desperate to see him, to make love with him, cuddle up with him by the fire and talk about their lives…

It was as she put her head under the water to let the water soak through her hair and over her face that it hit her: Why couldn't she have something with James? She didn't have to marry him or anything - after all, that would be illegal since she was still unfortunately very much married. But why couldn't she date him? Call him her boyfriend? Have fairly regular, mind-blowing sex with him? Even if - when - she moved back to Bristol. After all, it was only a couple of hours away. They could meet up regularly… and if it didn't work out, then she wouldn't risk bumping into him while shopping.

She sat up abruptly, water and suds flowing down from her hair. How had this realisation not hit her earlier? She had always equated leaving Totnes with leaving James, ever since they had started their flirtation three weeks or so previously. But she was realising now that it didn't have to be that way…

With this idea hitting her full force, she could no longer luxuriate in her foamy bath. She washed her hair and shaved as quickly as she could, before showering off the suds and wrapping herself in a big towel. She couldn't leave this for another two days - she needed to tell him now. Even if it was Christmas day. Especially because it was Christmas day!

Impatiently, she blow dried her hair, feeling like it was a very stupid idea to go out into the snow with dripping hair (not to mention what James might think of the look). When it was finally dry, she applied her make-up with more precision than the hair drying had been afforded, and slipped into her tight black jeans, a long sleeve top and her Christmas jumper - a dark navy blue with a glittery snow scene on the front, including Father Christmas flying across the sky.

By the time she was ready she felt like a nervous wreck; she couldn't help but wonder what his response would be to her suggestion that they could carry on like they had been for this week well into the New Year. Perhaps, with her moving back to Bristol, he wouldn't be interested…

Knowing she would just question every possibility until she knew for sure, she headed downstairs and out to her car, where errant snowflakes were still falling from the sky and landing on windscreens and gardens. Although the ground was white, there wasn't yet enough snow to make travelling difficult, and once Lee had managed to remove the snow and ice from every window and mirror on the car, she was able to travel the couple of miles with relative ease.

Her heart was hammering the whole way, and she distracted herself by looking at the Christmas light displays in windows, on rooftops and in gardens as she drove past. They all looked even more magical with that sprinkle of snow on top of them.

As she made her way up the lane to James' house, she forced herself to focus on the words she was going to say, to stop herself from backing out. There was something so vulnerable in what she was trying to say - yes! Let's give it a go! - that she felt like she might be opening herself up for heartbreak. But, she reasoned with herself, if she didn't open herself up to it then she'd miss out on the happiness too.

Snowflakes fell onto her hair as she stepped out of the car, and she blinked rapidly to try and dislodge a snowflake that had managed to fall onto her eyelash. Nervously, she rapped on the front door - and waited.

He answered the door in black jeans and a white shirt that was open at the collar. Lee felt her mouth go dry and she struggled to find the words that had been there only minutes ago.

“Lee!” James said with a grin. “I didn’t expect to see you today. Are you okay?”

She nodded, swallowing slightly and shutting her eyes for a second. “I need to say this, so please just let me get it out,” she said, and he didn’t voice the million questions that were inside his head.

“The last three weeks have been amazing. The sex is bloody fantastic. And when I’m with you… I forget about everything that’s wrong or bad and I’m just… happy. I have to move back to Bristol next week - I’ve got a career to go back to. But… I was hoping that, maybe, we could give us a go. Properly. With perhaps a little hint of commitment.” She took a deep breath, glad she’d said the words, and let her eyes rise to meet his. His cheeks were red, with the cold she presumed, and he looked a little lost for words himself.

“You want to date? Properly? As in you’d be my girlfriend, I’d be your boyfriend, not just casual hooking up?”

“I’d like to give it a go,” she said with a nod. “I know I’m a bit damaged - I’m warning you that now. But James… you make me happy.”

James’ hands went roughly to her waist, and she almost fell in his eagerness to pull her closer to him. Their lips crashed together and Lee - taking the gesture for a yes - wrapped her arms around his neck and pulled herself even closer, letting her tongue explore his lips, his mouth, as she tried to hold back a groan of want.

“James?” a voice called from inside the house. “You’re letting all the cold air in. Who’s there?”

Their chests rising and falling rapidly with the exertion of the kiss, they broke apart and Lee glanced at James. His lips moved to behind her ear, where he kissed before whispering: “As much as

I'd love to seal this deal by taking you upstairs and ravishing you - and yes, I agree the sex is fantastic - my whole family are just in the other room."

"Oh, God," Lee said, putting a hand to her head. She couldn't believe her stupidity. "I forgot! It's Christmas Day, I knew you were with your family… how could I forget! And now I've announced how good you are in bed to your family, I bet… I'm mortified." Her cheeks burned bright red, and it certainly wasn't just because of the cold.

"Oh, I'm sure they didn't hear that bit, don't worry. Come in - I'll try not to make it obvious that I want them to go home so I can take you upstairs."

Lee giggled. "I can't. It's Christmas Day. You go, be with your family - I'll see you when I see you."

"Lee," he said, grabbing hold of her hand and pulling her in close once more. "The only reason I didn't invite you is because I thought it would freak you out about me wanting more than just something casual. I want you to come in. Please." She couldn't resist that look in his eyes, and indeed she didn't get much choice - still holding her hand, he stepped into the cottage and closed the door. "There," he said, brushing the snow from her head and taking her coat from her. "That's better. Come and meet everyone."

Lee took a deep breath and, hand in hand, followed James into the living room.

Lee wouldn't have been surprised if James could feel her nerves somehow; he gave her hand a little squeeze as they entered the living room.

"Hey, guys, this is Lee. Lee, this is my mum, dad, my brother Jack, my sister Therese, and their wives Janet and Tamsin."

Lee raised her hand, feeling a little awkward. “Hi - Merry Christmas!”

His family greeted her in the same way, with all the festive tidings - but she could still see their slightly questioning looks at James.

“Lee’s my girlfriend,” James said, a silly grin on his face that he couldn’t wipe off. He turned to look at Lee, and saw that she was grinning too; a slightly awkward smile, but a smile all the same.

“Girlfriend!” James’ mum said, piercing Lee with a stare. “Well, it’s the first we’ve heard of it! Come and sit over here love, let me make sure you know what you’re getting yourself into with this one. James, go and get your girlfriend a drink, for goodness sake.”

“Yes mum,” James said; with a laugh, Lee also did as she was told and went to sit next to his mum. Although her hair was greying, her face had a youthful look to it, and the bright green glasses wouldn’t have looked out of place on someone much younger.

“So, I’m afraid I’ve heard nothing about you!” Mrs Knight said.

“It’s all quite new,” Lee admitted, not letting on quite how new - she didn’t need to know they’d only really become a couple in the last ten minutes. Nor that they’d made love on that carpet right in front of the fireplace…

“Ah, I see. Don’t you try to cover for my son, I’ll be having words with him about keeping you hidden away. So, what do you do, Lee?”

"Don't grill her, mother!" James said, re-entering the living room with a large glass of wine for Lee.

"I drove," she said quietly in his direction, glancing at the glass. He tilted his head to one side and shrugged with a cheeky grin, passing the wine to her anyway. Clearly he didn't plan on her going home that evening.

Lee turned back to his mum and tried to answer her question. "I'm a lawyer, in Bristol," she said, trying not to react to the shocked looks on their faces. "But I've been down here for the last six weeks setting up a café."

"A café! My, what a career change. And you're staying here?"

"Mum…" James said in a warning voice.

"I'm not sure yet," Lee said honestly. "But I do love it."

"Well of course you do," James' dad chipped in. He had a full head of hair that was a dark grey, and he was tall and slim with the same piercing blue eyes as James had. "Best place to live in the world, Devon."

"I'd have to agree," Lee said. "I have to admit, I've fallen in love with the place." She caught James' eye; he was definitely a bit part of her attraction to Devon…

"Have you eaten?" James asked, and Lee shook her head.

"But don't worry, I'll be fine."

"Don't be silly - we're having our Christmas lunch at four. Can you come and give me a hand in the kitchen for a second?" Lee nodded and excused herself, wondering if he wanted to speak to her or whether he was just giving her a reason to not be interrogated by his family.

"I'll have another cup of coffee please, James," his mum said.

"Ooh, me too," said his sister, and before long multiple drinks orders were placed.

"Good job I've got practice in remembering drinks orders," Lee said with a grin as they headed to the kitchen.

The second the kitchen door closed, however, the thoughts of drinks orders were promptly forgotten as James turned and pressed her back up against the door, his fingers combing through her hair and his lips crushing against hers. It took her brain a second to catch up, but when it did she felt her body mould into his and could have sworn his heart was beating as fast as hers. The hardness of his chest was pressed into her and she wrapped her arms around his waist, revelling in the warmth that this kiss brought her.

She didn't know how long it was before he broke away - only centimetres though. His lips hovering above hers, his breath as ragged as hers, he murmured: "Thank you."

"What for?" Lee asked, looking puzzled.

"For saying you want to give this a go. For coming round on Christmas Day."

"Oh," Lee said, letting the words settle in. "You're welcome. And thank *you* for that kiss…"

He pressed his lips to hers once more, then stepped away, taking hold of her hand instead. "Oh, there's plenty more where that came from - you can stay the night, I hope?"

"If you'll have me," Lee said with a raise of her eyebrows.

James grinned at the words. "Oh, Miss Davis, I will most definitely have you."

They were interrupted at that moment by James' brother walking through the door. Lee thought it was probably a good thing; his words had sent such a frisson of electricity through her that she wouldn't have been at all surprised if they'd had gone well beyond kissing without even thinking of the family members next door.

"I came to see if you need a hand," Jack said. "But I can see you haven't even got the kettle on yet." He had a knowing grin, and Lee looked away, blushing and trying to avoid eye contact. Her lips tingled where they had so recently been on James', and she felt sure that anyone looking at her would be able to tell that she had been so thoroughly kissed.

"I'm getting there bro," James said with a good natured grin. He let go of Lee's hand and headed to the kettle, leaving her under the scrutinising eye of Jack Knight.

"So, Lee," he said; Lee could see James straining to hear what he was saying over the noise of the kettle boiling. "You seem to have my brother all in a daze."

It was an odd statement, and Lee didn't quite know what to say; she felt in a daze herself.

"I hope you realise what a good guy he is." Ahh, it was the protective speech - she got it now. She'd given it herself before to suitors of Beth's that she hadn't been sure were quite in it for the right reasons. She guessed she was now that suitor - in Jack's eyes at least.

"I definitely do," she said, with a smile. "And I'm all in a daze as well." It seemed to be the right answer; Jack relaxed and began to ask her about how the café was doing. Together, the three of them carried the drinks into the living room and passed a pleasant hour sharing family news, with Lee listening in.

* * *

Christmas dinner was a noisy and extremely enjoyable affair. The table was laden with a roast turkey, stuffing, vegetables of all types, Yorkshire puddings… Lee couldn't even contemplate all the food that there was. Even though Lee had been a last minute addition, she was in prime position next to James and was served first. There certainly was enough food, even with an extra adult, and they all piled their plates high and tucked into the feast.

Conversation dwindled a little as the hungry guests ate, and Lee found she enjoyed the big family feel, as well as the amazing Christmas dinner that James had cooked.

"I never knew you could cook like this," she said as she took a break to let her food settle.

"Mum helps with a lot!" James said.

"Oh, don't you listen to him, he's a great cook. Always has been - used to help me when he was younger. Do you cook, dear?"

"Not much, I'm afraid, although I'm not too bad at baking. I've not really had the time to cook regularly in years, and I haven't ever actually made Christmas dinner!"

"Ah well, James probably wouldn't have done if he didn't live here. This cottage is just perfect for Christmas - that's what my mum used to say. And so with James living here, it just made sense for Christmas to be hosted by him! Not that he got a say in it really."

James laughed good-naturedly, and topped up Lee's wine glass before offering the bottle round the table. His sister and her wife, whose names Lee realised she had forgotten, accepted while the others passed. She presumed, since the cottage only had two bedrooms, that they couldn't all be staying over, and so some of them at least needed to be driving.

"How's work then, Therese?" James asked, addressing his sister, and Lee made a mental note to try to remember her name.

"Oh, you know. I work too many hours, too much marking, the usual." She rolled her eyes, then grinned. "But the nativity went well, and I only had to read the lines for one donkey with stage fright, so it was a good end to the term. Not a dry eye in the place when they sang at the end!"

"What age do you teach?" Lee asked.

"Year three - so seven and eight year olds. They get a lot of the big parts in the nativity - it's a lot of responsibility!"

Lee nodded as though she understood, although her experience with children was so limited that she didn't think she'd been to a nativity performance since she'd been in one herself.

Conversation lulled again; this time Lee thought it was probably because they all were so full they were exhausted. It was fairly quiet until Jack cleared his throat and the family turned to face him.

"While we're all together," he said, "Janet and I have some news." Janet was grinning next to him; a pretty brunette with long curly hair and dark purple glasses, she hadn't said a lot so far that day and so Lee hadn't really focussed much on her. "Janet's pregnant - we're having a baby in July!"

Silence for a second, and then a cacophony of sound; congratulations, questions, tears from James' mum, hugs all round. Lee said the right words - or she thought she did, it was all a bit of a blur - but she couldn't help feeling a little stunned. That reminder of what she had been working towards all these years yet again; the reminder of something that was now so far out of her reach. As exciting and exhilarating as these new feelings were, she knew there were always going to be times that reminders of her old goals, her old hopes and dreams, hit her square in the face.

When she felt she could do so without being rude, Lee excused herself to go to the bathroom and locked the door behind her. She took a few deep breaths, remembering the calming techniques from the yoga classes she had attended many moons ago in Bristol. She stood in front of the sink, and looked at herself in the mirror, trying to think positively. "You are not old," she told herself. "You can still have children. It's just 'later'. Not 'never'." She took a few more deep, calming breaths - in through the nose and out through the mouth. Things became a little clearer, her heart slowed down, and she realised how worked up Jack and Janet's happy announcement had made her.

"That's enough," she told herself. She could not get so upset over every pregnancy or child related announcement. Things happened for a reason; she could wait to have kids. She splashed cold water over her face, trying to make sure she re-joined the group looking normal, and not like someone who'd had an overreaction to a stranger's pregnancy announcement. Hoping for the best, she exited the bathroom.

*   *   *

Puddings, pies, charades and several hours later, James' assembled family decided it was time to head home. Having text Gina that she wouldn't be back that night, Lee had settled in for a fun, family Christmas evening - and found she had enjoyed it far more than she would have imagined, considering almost everyone there was a new acquaintance for her.

"Do you need a lift anywhere, Lee?" Mr Knight asked; Lee shook her head.

"No, thank you for offering though - I've got my car."

Thankfully, no-one commented on the fact that she had obviously drunk at least one too many glasses of wine to drive home, and that there was no way James would have ever let her drive home after too many drinks. Lee was glad; she didn't really want his lovely family to think about her staying the night with their son.

"Ooh, would you look at how much snow has settled!" Tamsin said as they stepped into the cold night air. "Haven't seen that here for years!"

"Make sure you drive carefully - watch for anyone driving erratically, or where you might skid."

"Yes, James," she said, with a roll of her eyes and a hug for him. "Thanks for having us!"

Compliments for the food, congratulations for Janet and Jack, wishes of a Merry Christmas and 'nice to meet you's to Lee filled the air, and Lee and James stood out in the snowy garden until the two cars had driven off slowly down the drive, leaving dark black tarmac in their wake, which was quickly being filled by freshly falling snow.

A misty aura hovered in front of the full moon, blocking the light a little but making it seem even more mystical in the process. Lee found herself drawn to it, watching as the clouds were slowly blown over it; the whole world went darker for a few seconds until it was revealed again. She remembered clearly being a kid and convincing herself she had seen Father Christmas flying across a similarly bright moon one Christmas Eve when she'd been seven or eight. She smiled at the memory; the magic of Christmas had always been strong. She'd thought, when she fled Bristol six weeks ago, that this would be the worst Christmas ever… now she wasn't so sure. It was definitely different - so much had changed in those six weeks - but it most certainly wasn't all bad. It might be the most unusual Christmas yet - but she definitely didn't think it was the worst.

James' arm snaked around her waist, and she leant her head on his shoulder, shivering slightly in the snow but enjoying the magical feeling of a white Christmas. James began to hum the old Christmas tune, and she smiled and turned to face the voice, then whipped her head back round - out of the corner of her eye, she could have sworn she'd seen something fly across the moon…

"What's up?" James asked, looking confused.

"Nothing…" Lee said. "Just a bit of Christmas magic, I think."

CHAPTER EIGHTEEN

When Lee woke up on Boxing Day morning, she didn't wonder where she was. Although she had only spent one night in this bed previously, she found herself waking up with James curled around her, and as her eyes flickered open and spotted those exposed wooden beams on the ceiling, she felt completely at peace with the world.

For several minutes she didn't move, but soaked in the feeling of being held in James' strong arms, against his muscled, bare chest. She revelled in the sensations, resisting the temptation to run her smooth legs against his athletic calves; as much as she wanted to feel him against her, she wanted to let him sleep for a little longer. Last night… last night had been incredible. A few too many drinks, that was for sure; a passionate night that had begun with wine, ended with champagne, started in the kitchen, then the bathroom, then up to the bedroom… Lee almost blushed at the places round the house that their clothes were sure to be found.

She knew that James had to work a shift from three that afternoon, and a hangover certainly wouldn't help him with that - let alone a lack of sleep. But the temptation to stroke his face, his hair, to wrap her arms around his waist was strong.

It wasn't long before his eyes flickered open, and when he saw Lee's eyes open and watching him his lips split into a wide grin.

"Good morning," she said. "I hope I didn't wake you."

James shook his head. "No, don't worry - how're you feeling?" Lee knew he must be referring to the alcohol they'd consumed the night before.

"Not as bad as I was expecting - although I've not attempted to get out of bed yet!"

“I wish we didn’t have to,” James said, and he smiled that smile that made Lee’s heart flutter inside her chest.

“It’s already ten o’clock though,” Lee said, “And you’ve got work this afternoon!”

James pressed his face into her shoulder, his breath tickling slightly and causing her to giggle. “If we could stay in bed all day, I would,” he said.

“Christmas wishes were yesterday,” she said - but for once she wasn’t feeling any Boxing Day blues after her favourite holiday of the year was over. No, far better than any Christmas presents was the knowledge that she’d made a decision about James - and the excitement in her chest when she thought of continuing some sort of relationship with James made her sure that she had made the right decision.

“Come on - I’ll make you breakfast.” Lee sat up, and then remembered she was totally naked - and had no clothes anywhere in reach. As at peace with the world as she was feeling, she wasn’t quite ready to walk naked in front of a man she had slept with a handful of times. She blushed, and turned to James. “Have you got anything I can wear?”

James grinned, and leant over to a side drawer next to his bed. Lee grinned as she glimpsed his bare bum beneath the sheets, and he passed her a t-shirt and a pair of his boxers.

“Thanks.” She managed to slip into them without losing any dignity, she was fairly sure, and padded softly across the bedroom carpet, downstairs to the kitchen. She smiled to herself as she saw the Christmas tree, with two new ornaments added: the felted black dog, and the delicate glass ballerina. It had been last night, after his family had left and before they’d consumed the last of the champagne, when James had reached under the tree and presented her with a small, blue and silver package. She opened it excitedly, and when that same glass ballerina that had sparked their conversation in the garden centre had rolled out, she'd nearly had tears springing to her eyes. When she pulled the tiny parcel out of her handbag and handed it to him, his look of surprise when the felted dog ornament was revealed made her laugh. She was amazed that both of them had had the same idea – and that neither had spotted the other! James had immediately hung his on the tree, and since Lee wasn't planning on heading home that night, hers had joined it. Now, in the morning light, they still glinted with a little of the magic of the night before.

Whilst she was certainly no great cook, she thought she could whip up something semi-decent for breakfast, and she began to rummage in the very full fridge to see what her options were.

Cooking in the strange kitchen certainly took longer, as she searched for a jug and came back with colander, but twenty minutes later she was fairly pleased with the two plates of scrambled eggs and bacon on toast that she had assembled. She checked a few drawers for a tray, as there was no way she could carry it all upstairs without dropping it, and finally found one on top of the fridge. Laden with the plates, two cups of coffee and cutlery, she ascended the stairs carefully and nudged the bedroom door open with her foot.

At first glance, she thought James had fallen back to sleep, but on feeling her sit down on the bed his head lifted a little - and he grinned when he saw what she was carrying.

"I didn't think you were actually going to bring me breakfast!" he said, sitting up carefully to avoid knocking the tray.

"Where did you think I was?"

"I don't know - shower? Run away after being grilled by my crazy family?"

Lee grinned and began to cut into her food, surprised she could be hungry at all after the massive feast they had eaten for their Christmas dinner. "Ah, they're not so crazy."

"I'm sorry they asked so many questions," James said, in between mouthfuls of food. "I know they can be a bit… intense."

"They care about you - that's not so bad, is it?"

James smiled and rolled his eyes, wolfing down the rest of his breakfast. "Mmm, that was just what I needed. Thank you…" He leant over and kissed her on the lips, not caring that she hadn't yet finished her breakfast.

"That'll teach you to drink too much on Christmas day!" Lee said putting both their plates on their floor and curling up in the crook of his arm, letting out a deep sigh. James placed a kiss on the top of her head.

"If getting drunk on Christmas day leads to sex all over the house and breakfast in bed - I'm afraid you're not doing a great job at putting me off."

* * *

Outside the snow had stopped falling, and although everywhere was a frosty white, Lee thought it looked safe enough to drive. The radio news she'd listened to while she'd cooked breakfast had said there was likely to be more snow later in the day, but for now the sky was a cloudless blue. In front of them, Lee and James' breath swirled in a cloud of smoke, and those clouds met as they moved in for one more kiss.

"I'll see you tomorrow - our beach date, remember?" Lee said.

"I know… drive safely, okay?"

Lee nodded, and pulled him down for another 'one more' kiss. "If you want to come round after you've finished… you're welcome."

"I don't even have your address!" he said, and she promised to text it to him once she was home.

They drove off in convoy, James insisting on leading the way in case the roads were icier than he'd initially thought. He hooted as he went off towards Kingsbridge, where he was working that day, and Lee drove slowly through the sleepy town centre, where most people were still snugly burrowed away in their houses.

The flat door was not enough to stop the Christmas music that was blaring inside, and Lee shook her head with a grin and unlocked the door. Gina was dancing round the living room in her pyjamas, a Christmas classics CD playing and a mug of coffee being danced around with rather dangerously.

Lee watched for a few minutes, feeling amused by her flatmate's lack of inhibitions, before clearing her throat. When that wasn't heard, she shouted: "Hey!"

Gina jumped, then smiled when she saw who it was and lowered the volume of the music. "Hey! Sorry, just enjoying the Christmas spirit for another day."

"If I didn't know better, I'd say you had been imbibing a little too much Christmas spirit!"

"Nah, that was last night - especially when I came back to a cold, empty flat!"

"Sorry, sorry - I drank too much last night too, if it's any consolation."

"Details, please!"

"Coffee, please!"

"Deal."

Coffees in hand, they settled on the sofa and Lee shared a few choice details from her Christmas day.

"And so I decided that, here or not, I want to give whatever this is between us a shot. So we're going to date - here, Bristol, wherever - and see what happens."

"I'm pleased for you, Lee," Gina said, sipping her coffee. "You seem so happy - I didn't understand why you were planning on it being a finite thing. Now I just need to persuade you to stay here…"

Lee didn't answer; she'd given every answer she could to that one, and she didn't want sadness about leaving to tinge the remaining time she planned to spend here. Besides, it wasn't like she was never coming back…

"I met his family, too," she said, sure that that piece of information would distract Gina. "And the night ended with our clothes littered across his house!" She blushed, but knew for definite that Gina would be hooked by *that* one.

"Get you!" Gina replied. "Is he good in bed? You can tell he'd be muscled under that uniform…"

"I'm not giving you all the details - but I certainly haven't been disappointed!"

"Lucky cow."

Lee couldn't remember the last time she'd had such an open, entertaining discussion about her love life. She guessed that there hadn't really been enough sex in recent months with Nathan for it to be a topic of conversation - and they weren't exactly the kind of chats she had at work. She couldn't remember when she'd last socialised outside of work, either… not before coming here.

"Anyway, I was going to cook Christmas dinner yesterday - but then I ended up eating at James'. So I thought I'd cook it today, for the two of us, if you're up for it?"

"Second Christmas dinner - yes please! We've got a bottle of wine in the fridge too, that'll help shift the hangover!"

"I'm not promising much," Lee said. "I've never actually cooked a Christmas dinner! But I'll give it a go."

Soon the Christmas music was back on and Lee had changed out of her clothes from the day before into a fresh pair of jeans and a long floaty top. She shoved her hair up out the way and entered the kitchen to start getting food ready. The turkey she knew needed to go in early - when she checked the timings, she realised she had underestimated somewhat. "It might be eight o'clock by the time this is ready!" she shouted through in warning to Gina - but she wasn't sure if she was heard over the loud Christmas music.

Humming along to the tune, she began to chop vegetables and potatoes, before remembering she hadn't texted James her address. It would be nice to see him… perhaps he'd stay here the night. She presumed Gina wouldn't be bothered!

As she grabbed her phone from her coat pocket, which was hung on the rack in the hallway, there was a knock at the door. "Turn it down Gina!" she shouted - but the volume didn't change, so she presumed she was unheard again. She opened the door, fully expecting it to be a neighbour complaining about the noise - and nearly shut it again in shock.

There in front of her, his dark skin contrasting against his light grey coat, was Nathan. There were flecks of snow in his hair, and he wore a slightly pained expression, although he smiled when she met his eye.

"Hi, Lee. Happy Christmas."

She was shocked on so many levels, and a myriad of questions ran through her mind. Why was he here? How did he know where she lived? Why did he have to come now, when she felt happy, when she was moving back to Bristol in a few days?

"Nathan," she finally said, unsure which of these questions was the most important. "How did you know where I live?" It was blunt - but it was the one that was bothering her the most.

"Your mum," he said with a shrug. "I went round there, begged her to give it to me - she didn't want to, so don't blame her."

"Why are you here?" It seemed odd that she was speaking to the man she had been married to, the man she had loved, the man she had thought she had known everything about, in the hallway of a block of flats, and in such staccato sentences. But that was where they were.

"I need to talk to you Lee - can I come in?"

Part of her wanted to say no; to protect her little haven from the negativity that surrounded him in her mind. But she knew she couldn't, and so she let him in, watching as he screwed his face up to the deafening blast of Christmas music. She felt like she was betraying herself to do so, but she scurried into the living room and switched it off.

"Hey!" Gina said, turning to scowl at her. "I was listening to that!"

"Nathan's here..." Lee said, raising her eyebrows and opening her eyes wide. Gina's eyes widened too and her mouth formed an o.

"I'll scram," she said, grabbing a half-eaten packet of crisps from the table and taking it with her to her bedroom. Before she closed the door, she turned round and whispered: "Are you okay?"

Lee nodded, although she wasn't sure if that was the truth, and the bedroom door shut. And then Nathan was there, in the living room, having taken an inordinately long time hanging up his coat; she guessed he'd heard her having a conversation.

"Do you have company?" he asked, glancing around the living room. She could almost see him judging the brightly coloured throws and the mis-match of furniture.

"Just my flatmate," she said, sitting down on the sofa without offering him a seat or a drink. He sat down anyway. "Why are you here, Nathan?" She could hear the exhaustion in her voice; she'd had enough of these feelings, enough of feeling upset and confused over the way her life had panned out. She'd made a decision to move on - and him turning up here certainly wasn't helping.

"I made a huge mistake, Lee." He reached across the sofa to take her hand, but she moved it from his reach; she wasn't ready for that. He carried on regardless. "I'm sorry. So sorry. I see now I was an idiot - just thinking that the grass was greener. What we had was good, and I ruined it all. Please, Lee - please say I haven't ruined everything."

Her head was reeling at these words; the words she had wanted to hear six weeks ago now felt hollow. She felt she had lived so much more freely, so much more happily - that his words didn't have the impact she would have expected.

“Nathan… you said you were seeing someone. You said you wanted a divorce.”

“I didn’t know what to do, when you just upped and left, started a whole new life here, or so it seemed. I’m not blaming you,” he said quickly as she opened her mouth to speak. “Just that I didn’t know how to deal with it. I’ve made some choices I’m not proud of, Lee - but I’m sorry. I love you. I want to be with you. I’ll even move here, if it’s what you really want.”

That one took her by surprised. Move to Totnes? She couldn’t picture him here, not in a million years. And the idea of him living in the same town as James… well, that didn’t bear thinking about. Were she even to consider a life with Nathan again, she knew it would not be in Totnes.

“Nathan. A lot has changed. You made your choices, I made mine. You screwed at least two other people during our marriage - I don’t even want to know if it’s more. I can’t just get over that.”

“Please, Lee.” He was on his knees now, on the floor, and Lee didn’t know where to look. He laid his head on her knee, and she thought for a moment that he might be crying. “Lee. Lee, I messed up, big time. I can see now how great our life was - and I don’t want to lose that forever. Please, please forgive me.”

They sat there like that for a few moments, and Lee felt frozen. Her mind wouldn’t work properly; she couldn’t think about his words, she couldn’t consider the possibilities they offered - she was just stuck in that moment, with Nathan by her feet, her whole world turned upside down yet again.

It felt like hours but Lee thought it could only have been ten minutes - if that. Nathan lifted his head, and his dark eyes met hers and she felt… nothing. Not the anger or hatred she’d felt for the last six weeks; not the love or passion she’d felt in the months and years before. She felt simply empty.

"I can't answer you right now," Lee said, knowing she couldn't think about any of these things while he was there in the room. "I need time. This is a massive thing that you're saying."

"Okay. Okay. I want you to think this through - I think you'll see that our life can be good again, if we really work at it. Great, I think it can be great. If you can forgive me… I'll make it up to you, I promise."

"Go back to Bristol, Nathan. I'll think about it."

"When will I hear from you?"

"I'm back on the second. I'll ring you - we can discuss it, okay? I will think about it." She felt she owed him that - although the second the thought crossed her mind, she chastised herself. She owed him nothing!

"Thank you. Thank you Lee…" He stood, and Lee did too; he bent his head to kiss her, and she moved her head so his lips lightly grazed her cheek. Neither commented on it; inside, Lee felt riled and a little sickened that he felt he could just kiss her again like nothing had happened. Kiss her like James had kissed her…

They walked in silence to the door, and Nathan stood on the threshold for a moment, looking at Lee.

"I love you, Lee. I want our whole life back; I want to live with you, I want to have kids with you, I want our marriage back."

And then he was gone; and Lee closed the door, slid her back down it and sobbed on the carpeted hallway floor.

CHAPTER NINETEEN

"Lee?" A soft voice came from the living room, followed by footsteps. "Oh, Lee." She sank to the floor and sat cross-legged next to Lee, trying to awkwardly put an arm around her. "I thought I heard the door close."

"Oh Gina," Lee sobbed, leaning her head against her friend's shoulder and letting her feelings and her tears pour out. "I was so sure I knew what I wanted, that I'd made the right decisions, made the best of all of this… and now… and now…"

"What's that bastard done now?" Gina asked, never one to mince her words.

"He says he's sorry. He says he loves me. He says he wants everything back again - that he wants children with me! I've waited for so long for him to be ready to have children with me, and now he turns up, tears in his eyes, says he got it all wrong and that he doesn't want to lose everything we've had…" She tried to wipe her tears away with the sleeve of her jumper, but they wouldn't stop falling. "And now my mind is so mixed up and I'm questioning everything I've decided."

"What a shit, coming in and throwing all of that at you on Boxing Day of all days. Come on - let's make that Christmas dinner together. We can talk through it all, see if we can figure out what you really want."

Lee nodded, and with a hand from Gina, got up onto her feet. She nipped into the bathroom to noisily blow her nose and splash some cold water on her face. It was as she headed back to the kitchen that she remembered she had been on her way to check her phone when the unwelcome guest had appeared at the door. She pulled it out of her pocket, and saw what she was hoping for and dreading at the same time. *New message: James.*

She clicked to open it and read the words with her breath held. *Still not got that address from you! That breakfast - and those kisses - have got me through an exhausting shift. See you later xxx*

She caught a glimpse of herself in the mirror and knew that she couldn't see James tonight: she looked a sight, her head was a mess and there was no way in hell that she could sit and cry over her separated husband reappearing and telling her he loved her with her new boyfriend.

I'm sorry, feeling a bit rubbish, just need an early night - can we rain check until tomorrow? Xxx

He replied almost immediately. *Can't say I'm not disappointed, but I hope you feel better. Looking forward to tomorrow - wrap up warm! J xxx*

She sighed as she placed the phone down on a side table and entered the kitchen to find Gina basting the small turkey.

"What a whirlwind of a Christmas," Lee said, as she began to chop the potatoes for roasting. "I can't believe he showed up like that."

"So," Gina said, pouring them both a sizeable glass of wine and piling vegetables into pans. "Truth time. What you need to decide is - do you want to forgive him? And do you think you can forgive him?"

"After it happened… once I was done being furious, and then devastated… those words were all I wanted to hear. I thought if he was just sorry, if he wanted me to forgive him, then we could move on. But then he came here, and he wasn't really apologetic, and he wasn't that desperate for my forgiveness. And then he dated someone else…" She put the knife down, realising she was chopping the potatoes far too aggressively and far too small, and decided to give up on a bad job and throw them into the oven with some olive oil and rosemary. "And now I'm dating someone else. The kindest, funniest, sexiest man I could have imagined. And I have felt so happy…"

"But?"

"But I have so much history with Nathan. We have a whole life together, a marriage, we know each other's parents, we were - or I was - ready to have children. And if I can't forgive him, then all of that is gone, forever."

"You can't blame yourself, Lee. Whether you forgive him or not, none of this was your fault. He made his horrendous decisions - he's responsible for the fall out."

"I don't know," Lee said, sipping her wine and beginning to make gravy. "Things were distant a long time before I walked in on him and *her*… We weren't having sex, we didn't spend much time together, it was all work, work, work. Maybe I can't blame him totally."

"And were you sleeping with gorgeous interns at your office? No, I didn't think so. Lee, listen to me. Things may have become a bit stale, the sex might have dried up, but what was needed was *conversation,* maybe therapy - not sleeping around. And that was his decision. If he didn't think things were working, he could have talked to you, he could have left you for Christ's sake - but he bowed out of the grown up decisions and got into bed with at least two workmates. The blame is most certainly squarely at his door." Feeling her speech had run its course, she took a large swig of her wine and opened the oven door. "Right, vegetables on, I think this will all be ready to eat in twenty minutes."

"Thanks, G - for everything. Dinner - and the words of wisdom. And… I think you might be right. But… but what about the future? The plan for having kids, the nice house, the life plan…"

"Screw the life plan! You can have kids for at least the next ten years Lee, probably much longer. You're not as old and on the shelf as you seem to have decided you are. You can start again, with someone else, and still have the amazing life you always dreamed of. Better, in fact, than before - because it wasn't exactly perfect, was it?"

"No. No it wasn't. And... and I'm struggling to see how I could possibly forgive him. Not any time soon. And even though it's only new, and I don't want to get into anything really serious right now - this thing with me and James feels great."

"I think you've got your answer Lee - but sleep on it. Go on that date with James tomorrow - see how you feel in the cold light of day, without Nathan crying in front of you. Not that I'll judge you, whatever you decide to do. Just make sure you do what's best for you, not anyone else." She topped up the glasses of wine; "Come on, lay the table, let's dish up this feast and then watch a feel good Christmas film, hey? 'Tis the season, after all."

* * *

It was another fitful night's sleep for Lee, one of many she'd had in that bed since leaving Bristol. James' face appeared many times, as did Nathan's. She had a dream where she was pregnant, but the face of the father was blurry, and when she woke up in a sweat she couldn't remember enough of the key details to analyse what it could mean. When she finally fell back to sleep, images of her office swam through her thoughts; one moment she was in her little café, the next she was sat in her office, and that sexist celebrity client from what seemed like a million years ago was in front of her. Then she was walking through her Bristol living room; then her living room with Gina.

It was five am when she woke up and decided that she couldn't face going back to sleep again. The café was closed for today, to be reopened tomorrow - and then Lee would work her last four days, before heading back up to Bristol and life as a lawyer. As she made herself a cup of coffee in the chilly kitchen, she asked herself the question: would it be a life with Nathan? Her dreams hadn't helped her to decide, and she knew that her beach date with James would only make her want to be around him more - that was what every moment with him did to her.

She curled up under a blanket, and only switched on their tiny Christmas tree lights. Sat in semi darkness, she looked out of the window at the frosty street, where the snow still hadn't melted and more still was forecast later that evening. She closed her eyes and pictured that warm fireplace in James' cottage.

Then she tried picturing herself in her home in Bristol, curled up with Nathan in front of the television. A baby asleep upstairs… and a tear fell from her eye before she even realised it was there. A beautiful picture… and yet she couldn't imagine it. She didn't think she had it in her to forgive him for not one, but two indiscretions - and that was the ones she knew about. She could see now, in the cold light of day, that he had only returned because he'd realised that the grass wasn't always greener. She had never during their marriage pondered whether the grass might be greener elsewhere - and yet now that she'd been forced into the other grass, she'd found so many positives there. A new business venture, a new friend, a new boyfriend… Even back in Bristol, she could keep hold of those things.

She couldn't be with a man she didn't love anymore; a man she couldn't respect.

Instead of waiting until she was back in Bristol, as she'd told him she would, she decided to write him a letter. She felt as though she needed to get the words out of her, get this decision made, and then move on with her life. She couldn't wait in limbo; he'd come, he'd asked for her back, and she'd decided to say no.

Nathan,

I know we had problems in our marriage before you cheated. We both worked too much, and we both took what we had for granted. It's too late now, to go back and change that; I cannot forgive you right now, and your cheating has made it impossible to try to put in the work that we should have both put in so long ago.

We both need to move on from this - and I hope I can forgive you one day. I'm filing for divorce in the New Year; I hope we can split things amicably.

May next year be better than this one.

Lee.

She rifled through the cabinet drawer until she found an envelope, wrote their old address on the front (she presumed he was still living there) and put it in the hallway ready to post.

As soon as it was sealed she knew she'd made the right decision; it felt like a weight had been lifted from her shoulders. It was time for a new year, and a new start - as Lee Davis, not Lee Jones.

CHAPTER TWENTY

At ten in the morning, as planned, Lee was waiting outside at the top of the high street for James to pick her up. She'd posted her letter on the way down, and was wrapped up warm as instructed, with her big winter coat, scarf and gloves. A few snowflakes whirled around her head, and she wasn't sure if they had been whipped up by the wind or were freshly falling. Some of the shops were opening today, although several remained closed for another day - the charm of a small town.

Lee grinned as the car pulled up against the kerb, and she had the door open before James had time to open it for her. Before any words left either of their mouths, Lee pressed her lips to his, fastening her fingers into his hair and letting all the desire she felt for him clear in those few seconds.

"Wow." Lee settled back into her seat, grinning at the effect her kiss had on him. "I was a bit worried, when you brushed me off last night, that you were having second thoughts but… wow."

"Nice to see you too," she said, and as he pulled away onto the road she glanced at him and took a deep breath. "I want to tell you something, but it's not easy for me. But I'm excited about whatever we're starting here, and I don't want to keep this from you."

"Okay… do I need to pull over?"

"No. Keep driving, it's easier that way. And I'm excited about going to the beach. So…" Another deep breath. "My ex-husband - or soon-to-be ex-husband - turned up yesterday. And he apologised, and begged me to forgive him and come back. He said he wants to have a baby with me, get our life back together, make everything right again…"

"So that's why you cancelled?"

“Yes. I’m sorry - I wasn’t in the right head space last night to see you, to talk to you. I needed to… process.”

“And now you’ve processed…” Lee could see his fingers tightening and relaxing on the steering wheel, his knuckles turning white every couple of seconds. “And you’re telling me you’re going back to him?”

“No! No, James. I needed to process everything he said - and I came to the conclusion that I have been happier here than I’ve been in a long time. Happier with you… I could never be with a man I didn’t love. A man I couldn’t respect any more. I’m ready - ready to move on.”

James didn’t speak for a moment or two, as he turned off the main road, down a narrow country lane. Then he pulled in to a lay by, switched off the engine and turned to face Lee.

“Thank you for telling me. I was worried, yesterday - I thought that maybe you’d changed your mind about wanting to date me, or that my family had actually put you off with their protective questions. But I understand why you couldn’t see me yesterday - and I’m exceptionally happy that you wanted to see me today!”

“James… you have made me so happy. And I have no idea where we’re heading, but I know I want to feel this happy for as long as I can.”

“Lee. I know you’ve just ended your marriage, and I know that kind of thing takes a long time to get over. But I don’t want to be any rebound - I’m all in this.”

Lee didn’t have the words to show him how she felt, and so she unbuckled her seatbelt, climbed onto his lap and let her lips do the talking - figuratively, that was.

*　　*　　*

After their brief interlude, they drove through the tiny village of South Milton, down windy lanes that made Lee glad she wasn't driving. Tall hedgerows were covered in snow, and it was only when they turned a corner and reached the brow of a hill that Lee got her first view of the sea.

It was a breath-taking sight.

"Wow," she said, as they descended the hill slowly, wary of any ice. The sea was an icy grey colour, looking both ominous and mighty as it rolled and crashed onto the sand. Out in the distance was a huge rock with a large hole in the middle, and the sea foamed and sprayed around it, occasionally cascading down having landed on a ledge or in a nook. "I can't believe I lived here for six weeks and not made it to the beach!"

They pulled up in the small car park and had to battle the winds a little to get the car doors open. James took her hand, and whispered in her ear; "You're crazy, dragging me out here in December when there's snow on the ground!" Lee laughed, and pulled him along, their scarves wrapped tight around their necks against the cold.

It was hard to talk with the noise of the wind and the sea, not to mention the hats and scarves they were wearing, and so they walked fairly quietly, holding hands and marvelling at the natural beauty around them. Halfway along the deserted beach, James stopped and pulled Lee towards him for a kiss that warmed her from head to toe, despite the weather.

"Best Christmas ever!" he said with a grin, and pulled out his phone to take a photo of them both, with the sea in the background. With a broad grin, Lee put her head next to his, and for the next photo she turned and kissed his cheek.

He was right - this definitely had not been the worst Christmas ever. The most unusual, the most surprising - and quite possibly the best.

It was on the way home, with the heating blasting and the windscreen wipers on to swipe away the snow that had started to fall, that he asked her. "What are your plans for New Year's Eve?"

"I haven't got any… yet." Neither spoke of the elephant in the room - the fact that she would be leaving the day after. She hadn't even had a chance to look for places to live when she returned, so she thought she would have to spend a few nights in a hotel - or perhaps with Gemma or Tania - while she sorted something out. New Year's Eve - that would be her final night in Totnes.

"Would you spend it with me?" She was surprised that he even sounded unsure; after the last few weeks, after spending Christmas day together, she thought her answer would be obvious.

"I'd love to."

CHAPTER TWENTY-ONE

The last day of the year, and it had its own kind of magic brewing - or so Lee thought. She woke up with anticipation; not quite as strong as that surrounding Christmas, but it was definitely there. She tried not to think about how she would spend New Year's Day packing, saying goodbye and then driving back to Bristol - that was the future. There was no good worrying about it now.

When James had suggested going to the big New Year's Eve party at the pub opposite Carol's Café - the one she had stayed in that first night in Totnes - Lee had felt it was the perfect end to her adventure. And when Gina said she was going to - well, it was the icing on the cake. She'd offered to open up alone as Gina would be in charge for the foreseeable future, until they could afford to pay someone else to help her manage the place, and so was up early before most of the town. Snow still lay everywhere, and as she walked to work - wanting to enjoy the scenery one last time - she smiled at the memory of the children (and big kids!) who had been sledding down the high street's steep hill the day before, when the snow had happened to fall deep enough and thick enough for it to be possible. It had been many, many years since that had happened according to the locals, and the cars had stopped driving up the hill for the day, allowing all who wanted to to join in the festive fun.

Now, however, the street was quiet as most people were still in bed. The shops weren't yet open, the Christmas holidays were still in full swing for the kids, and the town had a peacefulness about it.

She unlocked the door and set about the familiar tasks of getting the coffee machine ready, turning the till on and making sure the glasses and mugs were well stocked. Gina had done a decent amount of baking the day before, and so there were enough sweet treats in the store cupboard to stock the cake cabinet well.

As soon as she flicked the sign to open and unlocked the door, she felt a sense of sadness descend; when would she be back here, after today? She didn't know, and the thought was not a happy one.

A customer soon appeared to take her mind off this, however, and when she raised her head at the tinkling sound of the bell, she grinned.

"Val," she said, "Did you have a nice Christmas? I haven't seen you in a little while!" The ex-owner of the café took a seat, and Lee set about making her regular order.

"I did dear, thank you - did you? This cold weather's too much for me to be out that long, at my age!"

"It was wonderful," Lee said with a grin and a blush.

"Oh? What made it so wonderful?"

Lee finished the cappuccino with an extra dusting of chocolate and carried it over to where Val was sat. Since there weren't yet any other customers, she took a seat. "Oh, you know, the festive spirit and all that."

"Hmm, the festive spirit? I heard a rumour you'd spent it with James Knight and his family!"

"Where did you hear that?" Lee exclaimed - but she was grinning.

"A very reputable source - his mother!"

"Oh, okay then, yeah I did. It wasn't exactly planned, but that's how it turned out."

"Well you keep hold of him, dear - he's one of the very good ones. Don't get many like him anymore. Now, I'm here because of another rumour I heard - and not from James' mother. Are you leaving tomorrow?"

Lee nodded. "I'm afraid so. Reality calls..."

"Oh, nonsense, you can choose your own reality! Which reality do you want?"

That one threw Lee for a moment. Did she have a choice? And if she did - which one did she want? She was about to answer, when the front door opened and a family of three walked in.

"Sorry Val, I'd better-"

"You go, but think about what I've said. You're part of Totnes now, and it's part of you - that doesn't just go away when the clock strikes midnight!"

*   *   *

The words did stay with Lee, all through a busy day in the café (the last day of Christmas hot chocolates was proving very popular) and even while she walked home with Gina at the end of the day. *It's part of you* - that certainly resonated with her. She didn't think she'd ever felt as at home somewhere, ever felt as linked with a place as she did Totnes.

"Do you know what you're wearing tonight?" Gina asked, her breath forming wisps of smoke in front of her.

"I've got this long sleeved, lacy black dress I was thinking about - but it is quite tight, I don't know if it's a bit much!"

"It's New Year's Eve, and you've got a gorgeous figure and a date with a handsome cop. I don't think it'll be too much!"

Lee laughed. "What about you?"

"I've either got a red top with black jeans, or this dark green dress I picked up at the vintage place at the top of town last week. You know, the one that's always packed with stuff? I think I'll try both on - you can help me decide."

They spent a very enjoyable couple of hours getting ready together with music, wine and a running commentary on their clothing and make-up choices. As Lee curled her hair in the mirror, she found she couldn't remember the last time she had enjoyed the getting read part so much. Somehow the curls seemed to hold in her normally poker straight hair; whether it was Gina's curler, the Devon water or some kind of Christmas magic she didn't know, but she was grateful for it.

Gina walked into her room in an emerald green wrap dress, with long sleeves and a slight frill at the hem. It dipped low to show off her cleavage, and she'd paired it with a bold bronze necklace. "What do you think?" she asked. "Too much?"

"Perfect," Lee said, looking her up and down. "You look sensational. And as you said to me - it's New Year's Eve, nothing is too much! Don't forget we're walking down, so no killer heels!"

"I can walk in killer heels, unlike you."

"Yeah, yeah. You wouldn't mind if James stayed tonight, would you?" She hadn't asked him yet, but it made sense for him to stay - after all, taxis would be few and far between on New Year's Eve. Besides, she wanted him to stay. She needed to spend her last night living in Totnes with him.

"As long as you keep it down!"

"Mind out of the gutter please!" But she laughed anyway. She pushed the bedroom door closed so she could take off her jeans and t-shirt and shimmy into the tight black dress. It hugged every curve, with long black lacy sleeves that would hopefully keep the worst of the cold out. She straightened it out, zipped it up and looked at the effect in the mirror. She planned to pair it with some knee-high black boots that Gina had offered to lend her. The outfit made her feel great, and she stopped caring whether it was over the top - and just hoped James would love it as much as she did.

Gina was in the hallway, applying her make-up in the mirror that had the best light. She wolf-whistled when she saw Lee behind her, causing Lee to grin and blush.

"James won't be able to keep his hands off you - not that he ever can!"

"Oh behave. Can I borrow that red lipstick of yours?"

"Yeah, it's on my dressing table." Lee applied the lipstick carefully; it was brighter than she would normally go for, but Gina had suggested it since she was wearing an all-black outfit, and Lee had to admit the effect was striking. Her loosely curled hair fell around her face, and once she had slipped on the boots she felt ready for anything.

Carefully, she sipped the end of her wine, waiting for Gina to be ready. They had agreed to meet James, as well as Gina's friends Dan, Kelly and Lydia, at the pub.

Wearing a pair of killer black heels that Lee wouldn't have dared to walk downhill in, Gina appeared in the kitchen. "Right! Let's say goodbye to this year in style!"

* * *

It was, as Lee had been expecting, heaving in the pub. It seemed it was the key place for locals to celebrate the end of the year, followed by everyone piling into the street to sing Auld Lang Syne and welcome in the New Year. As soon as they entered, Lee spotted James sat in a booth by the door, chatting away to Gina's friends who had already arrived. She watched him for a moment, his blond hair freshly washed, his blue shirt highlighting the muscles that she knew very well. He laughed at something Dan had said, and then happened to turn his head. Their eyes met, and for a second Lee felt like the whole world, the whole busy pub, stood still around her. There was only her and him in that second - until Gina grabbed her arm and dragged her through the crowd to the booth.

"I'll get the drinks," Gina said. "What are you having?"

"Vodka and orange, please," Lee said, and while others placed their orders, she slid into the seat beside James.

"Hey."

"Hey."

The others on the opposite side of the table were chatting amongst themselves; Lee felt James' hand on her knee beneath the table and blushed.

"You look sensational," he said, and he leant in to kiss her in greeting - a kiss that would have definitely continued if they weren't both mindful of the company they were in.

"Thank you," Lee said. "You look great in that shirt too." Then, feeling surprisingly cheeky, perhaps because of the two glasses of wine she'd drunk while getting ready, she leaned in and whispered in his ear; "And I'm sure it'll look great on my bedroom floor too."

His eyes widened, and then he laughed, a deep throaty laugh that Lee could feel vibrating through her. "Oh, Miss Davis, I think I've met my match in you."

He was saved thinking of a dirty reply when Gina reappeared with the drinks, complaining about some guy pushing ahead of her in the queue. In the end she'd given him such a lecture that he'd apologised and paid for her round - so she wasn't too bothered about it after all.

The night seemed to pass in a blur of drinks, stories, kisses and, by eleven o'clock, fairly loud music.

"I think I'm drunk!" Lee said above the din, as she sang rather tunelessly along with the song.

"Me too!" Gina replied - but neither seemed too upset by that fact.

"We need to toast," Lee said, looking round the table to make sure they all had drinks. "Before it's midnight!"

Everyone raised their glasses, and looked to Lee to decide what they were toasting. "To friendship, to romance, to Totnes!" she called, unsure if they could hear her or not. They raised their glass too, and she thought they repeated what she did - and she drank to those three things that she had discovered in the last two months.

Suddenly, a voice was calling out over the PA system; "Ten minutes 'til midnight, ten minutes 'til midnight."

"Time to go outside," James murmured in her ear, and the feeling of his warm breath against her skin made her whole body tingle with desire. "Time to ring in the New Year."

"I thought this was going to be the worst year - the worst Christmas - of my life," Lee said, not sure if she was slurring slightly but carrying on regardless. "And then you came into my life James, and suddenly everything seems magical again. Thank you." And they were outside, under the cold, starry sky, and they were kissing.

“I think you’re drunk, Lee,” James said with a smile, as he traced a finger lightly down her nose and touched it to her lips.

“I think I am too. But that doesn’t make any of it less true.”

Hand in hand, they made it to the huge circle of Totnes residents who were stood at the bottom of the town, some of them right outside Carol’s Café.

“Ten, nine, eight…” Lee looked round at this town, at the people she had got to know, at this feeling of community, and felt her heart almost glow with love for it all. She felt James’ hand in hers on one side, and Gina’s on the other as they all linked up to welcome in the new year.

“Seven, six, five…” She’d left the Christmas lights on in the café so they could bring the last moments of Christmas cheer to the year, and she could see them twinkling across the road, lighting up the smiling faces around.

“Four, three, two, one! Happy New Year!” Lee turned to James and saw the fireworks in the sky reflected in his eyes.

“Happy New Year, Lee,” he said, and she didn’t have a chance to reply before his lips met hers and he dipped her back slightly in a heart-warming kiss as the sounds of Auld Lang Syne began to echo around them. She felt out of breath when their lips parted; James arms stayed around her waist and hers stayed around his neck, not caring who was around them or what they might think.

“I think I’m falling in love with you Lee,” James said; he didn’t take his eyes from hers, but raised his hand to stroke an errant curl away from her eyes. “I don’t want you to go.”

"I don't want to go either," she said, knowing it was the truth; knowing that every fibre in her body was against leaving this place and returning to her former life.

"Then don't?" It was a question, said with hesitation - but Lee found the answer on her lips almost instantly. Maybe it was the wine, maybe it was the vodka, making the words easier to say - but that didn't change the fact that there was only one choice she could take; only one choice that, in her heart, she knew would make her happy.

"Okay." She saw the shock in his eyes, she saw his expression freeze, and then her mouth broke into a huge grin. "Okay! Okay! I'll stay here."

"You will? Really?" James was smiling too now, a smile that lit up his eyes. "Lee, please don't say it if you don't mean it."

"I don't want to go. I have no home in Bristol, I don't want to return to my life there - so why am I? I'm happy here. I'm happy with you." She took a deep breath. "I'm falling in love with you, too, James."

In that moment, he lifted her, spinning her around as she giggled and laughed. Onlookers stared; Gina smirked; Lee felt like the breath had been taken from her.

Finally he put her back down, and she was sure the dizziness wasn't just from him spinning her. He took her head between his hands, and between kisses muttered the words: "Best. New Year. Ever."

Eager to know what happens next for Lee and James? Read on for a sneak-peek at the second novel of the series, 'Lawyers and Lattes'!

* * *

Chapter One

A new year, a new start, and one hell of a hangover. Lee's eyes blinked open and then quickly closed again as the light streamed in through the window and past her unclosed curtains. Her head felt a little like it was a spinning plate, about to be dropped; she took a deep breath and opened her eyes again. The year had certainly started off bright, with the morning sunlight casting beams of illumination across the floor that was littered with items of clothing. Lee blushed a little, remembering how they got there, not all that long after a midnight kiss at the bottom of the town.

She rolled over and grinned at the sight that greeted her, despite the nausea that made her feel a little like she were on a rolling ship. Lying in a shaft of sunlight, blond hair glittering, lay the handsome figure of James Knight. She placed a hand on his bare chest, knowing full well that he had contributed at least half of the trail of clothes on the floor and was therefore completely naked under the covers. This was the first time she had woken up with him next to her in her own flat, and she couldn't resist the urge to run a hand through his curly hair, with his head so close to hers on the pillow.

"Sorry," she murmured as his eyes flickered open. He reached out an arm to pull her closer, and she found his face nuzzled into her neck. "I didn't mean to wake you."

"I'm off today," he said into her neck, the warmth of his breath making her shiver slightly as it tickled her delicate skin. "So I've got plenty of time to catch up on sleep. How are you feeling this morning?"

"Awful, if truth be told. I didn't think I drank that much… but I'm not as young as I used to be!"

James pulled away slightly so he could see her face, and moved his hand to stroke several strands of hair away from her eyes. "I didn't think you'd drunk that much, either," he said. "A bit tipsy, maybe, but not particularly drunk." His brow furrowed, and Lee stroked it with the tips of her fingers, confused as to why he was so concerned.

"Don't worry, I'm sure I'll live, hangovers only get worse once you're over thirty - you'll find out soon enough!" He didn't laugh, and Lee felt an unease in the pit of her stomach that she didn't think had anything to do with the amount - or lack thereof - of alcohol she had consumed the night before.

James ran a hand through his hair. "Last night…"

"I don't think I can think of words to describe last night," Lee said with a shy smile.

"I meant before we got back here."

"So did I, cheeky! Well, partially…"

James cleared his throat. "You do remember the whole night, don't you?"

"Of course I do, like I said, I wasn't that drunk."

James regarded her for a moment or two, not saying a word, just meeting her gaze. "You're definitely staying?"

Ahhh, Lee thought, so that was what was worrying him. It was so sweet she couldn't resist pressing her lips to his for a moment, and when she pulled away she grinned at him. "I'm staying. You can't get rid of me now - even if I'm so old that a couple of glasses of wine give me a terrible hangover."

James' grin lit up his eyes and rivalled Lee's at that comment, and he rolled so he hovered slightly above her. "You are young, and gorgeous, and I'm not planning on getting rid of you any time soon," he said, and now it was his turn to press his lips to hers, and her turn to feel as though she might dissolve into the air right there and then.

"Lee?" a voice shouted at the door, accompanied by a hammering that Lee's head could really have done without. "Lee, are you decent?"

Lee pulled away from James and glanced at him, and shook her head. "No!" she shouted back. There was what sounded like a laugh from the other side, then Gina's voice floated through the door once more. "I've made coffee, so make yourselves decent and come and get it while it's hot."

Lee grinned, even though James groaned as he rolled off her. Her flat mate Gina had struck her straight away as funny, direct and someone who took no rubbish - and that was exactly what she had turned out to be. Even though they'd only lived together for just over a month, they'd slipped into an easy rhythm that Lee couldn't remember feeling with anyone she'd lived with before - be it parents, siblings, house mates or partners.

They both scrambled around for some clothes to throw on; Lee had the luxury of her own pyjamas whereas James had to get properly dressed after being ill-equipped for the impromptu sleepover. The smell of coffee greeted them as they approached the kitchen, and it took Lee a minute or two to decide whether the smell made her more nauseous or improved things. She decided on it being an improvement and slid into the nearest chair, wrapping her hands around a mug.

“Well good morning love birds,” Gina said with a self-satisfied smirk.

“Good morning Gina,” James said with a grin; Lee just rolled her eyes. Gina and James talked for a few moments about the fireworks the previous night, the chilly start to the New Year and when he was next working, before Lee’s brain kicked into gear; there were many people who needed to know about her snap decision, and one of the most important was sitting right in front of her. Waiting for a lull in the conversation, Lee felt James’ hand on her knee and smiled.

“So, Gina,” she said, deciding to address the issue head on. “I’ve made a decision.”

“You’re staying here forever and never leaving?” Gina asked, taking a bite of an apple and grinning at her own little joke.

“Well,” Lee said, meeting James’ eyes for a moment before turning back to Gina. “Yes, in a manner of speaking.”

“You’re staying?”

“If you don’t mind! I know it was only going to be temporary, and you were going to run the cafe, but we talked last night and I realised-”

“Of course I don’t mind! I’ve been waiting for you to realise you belonged here. I’m very glad you didn’t disappear back to Bristol before realising it. Well done James - I’ll chalk this one up to your influence!”

“Happy to take the credit,” James said, taking a swig of the coffee Gina had placed in front of him. “Happy about a lot of things, actually…”

Gina made fake sick noises in the background; Lee rolled her eyes and told her to act her age, all with a big grin on her face.

After telling Gina of her plans to stay in Bristol, Lee knew there was only a limited amount of time left before she had to tell the other people in her life: her partners and her mother. She did consider messaging Nathan, but decided against it. After all, what difference did it make to him, really? And did he have a right to know what was going on in her life?

She was nervous about telling them for a myriad of reasons. She felt dizzy herself when she thought about the changes her life had gone through in the last six weeks - she wasn't sure how she could expect anyone else to keep up. And somewhere deep inside her, where she wouldn't quite even acknowledge its existence, there was the worry that someone (okay, she knew who it was likely to be - her mother) would suggest that this was all some sort of rebound. That she was making a huge mistake with her life; that she would ultimately regret it.

She knew in her heart that she didn't believe that to be true; that what she was feeling right now definitely didn't feel like some fling that was designed to move her past her disastrous failed marriage. But the possibility of hearing those words aloud… She put off the phone call for another day.

* * *

The bank holiday had allowed her to leave the cafe closed and succumb to her hangover, but the second of the month rolled round cold and bright, the first day of the year to open her lovely little cafe. Carol's Cafe (as she had named it, after her grandmother) had been her first solace when she'd arrived in Totnes at the beginning of December, fleeing a broken marriage and a cheating husband. When she'd found out the place was in desperate need of being taken over, she'd done so without much thought - and everything had very much snowballed from there.

James had worked the night of the first and so she had spent the evening alone, lamenting in the ridiculous fact that she missed him at the same time as enjoying a girly evening with Gina and the full width of the bed to herself. The very early morning alarm hadn't been quite so welcome, but a hot shower and a large mug of coffee later and she felt ready to tackle the world. Gina was still asleep when she left - they'd decided a rota would be made later on in the week since they would both be running the cafe now - and Lee slipped out in her thick coat and paint-splat scarf, deciding to walk down the steep hill instead of being lazy and getting the car out. Besides, she very much hoped James might stop by at some point and offer her a lift…

It wasn't until she was halfway down the hill that she remembered with a disappointing jolt that James was meant to be working late that night… perhaps she wouldn't get to see him at all that day - not a happy thought.

Once the doors were unlocked, the familiar routine of setting up the cafe seemed to whiz by, and before long the doors were open onto a particularly sleepy looking high street. Lee couldn't blame the residents; if she hadn't been working she would definitely have still been asleep at this hour.

Her first customer of the day surprised her somewhat, for she hadn't been seen out and about this early in the morning since giving up that same cafe. Val, the previous lease owner and surprisingly sprightly elderly resident of Totnes, had a big grin on her face when she saw Lee.

"You didn't disappear at midnight then?" she asked.

"I decided you were right, Val," Lee said, beginning to make her a coffee without being asked. "You can make your own reality - and this was what I chose. So, I'm afraid, there's no getting rid of me for a while at least!"

"And does young PC Knight have anything to do with this sudden change of heart?"

Lee blushed, and turned to froth the milk. When she turned back, Val's piercing eyes were still on her, and she couldn't avoid answering. "Maybe," she admitted.

"Life in a small town Lee - nothing stays secret for long, I'm afraid, although I don't know why you'd want to keep it a secret!"

Lee shrugged, unsure if she could put her feelings into words, unsure whether she even wanted to share the emotion that was bubbling up inside her. "I don't want to jinx things," she finally confessed, and was a little taken aback when Val reached over and patted her on the hand.

"That's a load of nonsense, dear, if you don't mind me saying. You follow your heart and it won't matter if the whole town knows - besides, James has lived here long enough that he'll know full well that you can't keep anything from the town!"

Other customers appeared before Lee really had a chance to respond, but she smiled a little at Val's words and got on with making teas, coffees and hot chocolates, her worries about 'jinxing' the relationship certainly soothed a little.

The busyness of the cafe made the time disappear, and before she knew it Gina had arrived and they were slap bang in the middle of the lunch time rush, serving take-away teas and coffees to workers in nearby shops and offices, and plenty of cakes too. They had discussed serving hot food, as Val used to do when she owned it, but had decided it was probably better to walk before they could run. Besides, neither of them were particularly great cooks, and hiring anyone else wasn't on the cards at the moment.

Lee was busy cleaning the milk steamer while waiting for the coffee to grind when she heard the bell above the door jingle for what seemed like the millionth time that day. She didn't even turn her head to welcome the customer, trusting that Gina would do so; it wasn't until Gina cleared her throat in what seemed like an overly dramatic way that Lee turned to see who had entered.

She found herself grinning without even thinking about it, and saw that he was the same, and that burnt away a lot of the strange anxiousness she had been feeling for the last day or so.

"Hey," she said.

"Hey." Lee was vaguely aware of Gina busying herself making the next batch of coffees with the freshly ground beans, and she felt suddenly like an awkward teenager with her first boyfriend, unsure of quite what the right thing to say or do was. They both took a step towards the counter at the same time, so that it was the only thing between them. James leant over, clearly intent on kissing her, and Lee didn't need to think before she leant towards him too. Had she been thinking about the cafe full of customers around them, she might have considered their kiss a little too deep and a little too long to be so thoroughly observed - but her mind was not on such matters at that moment in time. No, it was on his lips as they pressed against hers, his hand as it touched against her cheek, the feel of his sharply creased uniform beneath her palm…

And then one - or both of them - remembered where they were, and they pulled apart with a blush from Lee and a hasty cough to hide his grin on James' part.

Lee felt as though the cafe had gone silent around her, and when she dared to peek past James' fine, uniformed form she found that she was right - everyone in the small cafe seemed to be looking at them or pretending they hadn't just been looking at them

For a second, Lee closed her eyes and then snapped them back to meet James'; seeing that a grin still played on his lips, she tried to let her embarrassment at being the centre of attention fade away and allow the tingling memory of that kiss to be the only thing on her mind.

Slowly the buzz returned to the cafe, and although Lee was fairly sure that buzz was now about her and James, she decided not to listen in.

"Sorry," James said, running a hand through his hair as he always seemed to when he was a bit unsure of himself.

"For making us the talk of the town?" Lee asked, but there was a twinkle in her eye as she said it.

"Couldn't help myself," he said.

"Well, I guess there'll be no keeping our relationship under wraps in this place anyway," she said, echoing the earlier wisdom Val had shared with her.

"Did you want to?" His eyebrows knotted together slightly, and Lee once again got the feeling that this man in front of her wasn't quite as confident as she might have imagined.

"I guess I'm just not used to everyone taking an interest in my romantic life," she said. "Other than when everyone I knew found out my husband had cheated on me, I guess. Sorry, sorry, dark joke." She felt amazed that she could make a joke - dark or otherwise - about something that, not long ago would have had her hysterically crying. She smiled to lighten the mood. "And you never have to apologise for kissing me."

"Good," James said, taking the coffee that Gina wordlessly handed to him. "Have you rung your partners yet?"

Lee took a deep breath. "No. I was going to tackle that tonight, since you're working late." Once the words were out, she realised that was based on an assumption that they would be spending the night together every night - something that they had never discussed. Just because she was moving here did not mean, she told herself, that she should treat this like a ready-made long-term relationship. That seemed like a recipe for disaster.

"I'm sure they'll understand," he said, glancing at the clock before sipping his coffee.

Lee laughed. "I'm not so sure they will. They thought I was having a breakdown when I came down here in the first place. But, it has to be done."

"I've got to head off in a minute," James said. "I'm sorry - I wanted to see you, but I've only got ten minutes before I need to be back at the station."

"Thanks for coming," Lee said, twirling a sugar packet in between her fingers.

"Thanks for the kiss, and the coffee."

"Happy to help." She giggled, and when James bent to kiss her on the cheek she felt a shiver go through her.

"See you tomorrow?" he asked, putting his hat on as he stood up.

"I'll be here!"

"I finish at four. I'll pick you up?"

"Always good to save my legs the walk home."

"And take you out - stop teasing me!" James said, replacing a wayward strand of her hair behind one ear before ducking out of the door. Lee watched him leave, watched him turn and wave through the window, watched him cross the road and walk towards his parked police car.

"You've got it bad," a voice behind her said, and it broke her reverie. She turned to find Gina, with her purple-tinted hair scraped up in a ponytail and her lip piercing bobbing as she laughed.

"Oh, shut up," Lee said, the smile not leaving her face.

"Honestly, if you didn't deserve to be so happy I'd think it was all rather sickening. I'll need to have words with young PC Knight… if he hurts you, he'll have me to answer to."

And even though opening up her heart so soon after having it smashed to pieces was the thing Lee had been most afraid of, she was fairly sure that James would not hurt her. And if he did, she almost felt sorry for him, having to face an angry Gina.

****

Thank you so much for reading *The Worst Christmas Ever?*! I love Christmas just as much as Lee does, and so writing this novel – with plenty of Christmas music in the background – has been a dream.

Devon, and the South Hams in particular, also has a special place in my heart. I was born and grew up in the South Hams, visiting Totnes and Dartmouth regularly. As a student at university, Totnes was where I took the train to when I came home, and it's still somewhere I visit every time I visit my parents. It has a special something to it that I've not come across anywhere else.

I hope you enjoyed *The Worst Christmas Ever?* and that you have the best Christmas ever. Rest assured, this won't be the last you'll hear of Lee – or the beautiful South Hams. I'd love to hear your thoughts on Lee's story – email rebeccapaulinyi@gmail.com and I'll be happy to reply! You can sign up for my newsletter at rebeccapaulinyi.com to get news of new novels, free stories and the occasional cute picture of my dog!

If you enjoyed this book, you can find the rest of the series on Amazon!

Lawyers and Lattes (mybook.to/lawyersandlattes)
Feeling the Fireworks (mybook.to/feelingthefireworks)
The Best Christmas Ever (mybook.to/bestchristmas)
Trouble in Tartan (mybook.to/troubleintartan)
Summer of Sunshine (mybook.to/summerofsunshine)

Happy reading!

Rebecca Paulinyi

Acknowledgements

Thanks to NaNoWriMo, for giving me the reason to write madly for a month. Thanks to Jenny, for incredibly detailed line-by-line edits. Finally, thank you to my husband, who always supports my writing and will let me miss our movie night when I need to keep typing.

Printed in Great Britain
by Amazon

63346186R00129